The Diary of a Regency Lady

Jane Fenwick

Quantum Dot Press

The Diary of a Regency Lady

Jane Fenwick lives Pendle, Lancashire, England. She studied education at Sheffield University gaining a B.Ed (Hons) in 1989 and going on to teach primary age range children. Jane decided to try her hand at penning a novel rather than writing school reports as she has always been an avid reader, especially enjoying historical and crime fiction. She decided to combine her love of both genres to write her first historical crime novel Never the Twain.

Jane has always been a lover of antiques, particularly art nouveau and art deco ceramics and turned this hobby into a business opening an antiques and collectables shop in Settle North Yorkshire. However her time as a dealer was short lived; she spent far too much time in the sale rooms buying items that ended up in her home rather than the shop!

Animal welfare is a cause close to Jane's heart and she has been vegetarian since the age of fourteen. For the last twenty years she has been trustee of an animal charity which rescues and re-homes cats, dogs and all manner of creatures looking for a forever home. Of course several of these Jane has "adopted"!

Although Jane was born in Yorkshire and now lives in Lancashire, she is particularly drawn to the North East Coast which she knows well; often visiting Whitby, Sandsend and Alnmouth for research purposes. When she isn't walking on Sandsend beach she is to be found in her favourite coffee shop gazing out to sea and dreaming up her next plot.

The Diary of a Regency Lady

Jane Fenwick

ISBN: 978-1-912882-78-6

First published by Quantum Dot Press,
an imprint of Utility Fog Press

Acknowledgements

I would once again like to thank my early readers for wielding their red pens with alacrity. Also, thanks to Edwin Rydberg at Quantumdotpress.com for his patience and expertise.

On some occasions I may have fictionalised or blurred some details for the sake of the story. In such places, the errors belong to me alone.

Contents

November

November 1st

Walk into Killinghall and purchase highly recommended book (Mansfield Park) which I know everyone else read ages ago but have only just got around to buying.

Have decided from now on, despite not knowing where the time will come from, to read more widely. Indeed, I have drawn up a list of periodicals, novels and poetry, which I will strive to read and then discuss with friends and acquaintances. This path I think will enable me to sparkle a little brighter when there is a lull in the conversation as there inevitably is from time to time when one lives in the country. Feel it important to broaden my mind; just because one is a married lady with three children it is no excuse to stagnate. However, see if a lady appears *too* clever it is unbecoming so will not read serious tomes of history.

After luncheon (cold but not by Cook's intent) settle to begin new book. Am called away to the garden almost immediately by Brown asking if I have a preference for where he should plant the new rose bushes. This takes much time as where I would like them is clearly not where he wishes to put them.

Query: Why ask in the first place if he is going to quibble?

In the end settle that three dozen be planted where he wants them and the other thirty six where I wish them situated (so they can be seen from the conservatory and not hidden at the bottom of the drive). By the time the issue is resolved am frozen to the bone and in need of reviving. Take a small sherry as unable to find port decanter.

November 2nd

As I am arranging the drawing room flowers Lady Violet Carstairs arrives. No doubt she has heard I was about this task and has come to give me the benefit of her advice. Ask her to take a seat while I put the finishing touches to the arrangement. Pleased with the finished effect I stand back to admire it.

Lady V frowns and suggests bronze chrysanthemums should, in her humble opinion, be placed front and centre. Do I know she asks that the addition of a bowl of fruit and a pewter jug would make the arrangement just like a Dutch still life? Nod sagely and say after she has taken her leave I will indeed add the aforementioned items to complete the picture. In the meantime move bronze chrysanthemums to more prominent position - for now.

Lady V stays to tea. Do I realise says Lady V, that husbands are best ignored and completely surplus to requirements when one has produced an heir? How she knows this am unsure as she 'lost' hers some years ago. Think of several uses I could put Spencer to even though we have an heir and a spare but do not think it pertinent to share these with Lady V. Assure her I could not possibly do without my Beloved Husband under any circumstances.

We talk about the servant problem, Lady V's hothouse, remedies for toothache and the vicar's Sunday sermon when he appeared to have forgotten we all had homes to go to. Lady V enquires after the children - this only so she can then ask further about Spencer. Tell her the dear children are well, in detached tone. Then, so she doesn't think me foolish about BH, say he is as always in robust good health.

Query: Is it an untruth when he is abed nursing a sore head?

As Lady V takes her leave say what a pleasure her visit has been and how I hope we shall meet at my Dear Sister Hattie's house party on the morrow. Am gratified by the fleeting look on Lady V's face which tells me the Duchess must have forgotten to send the lady an invitation.

Note: Rock cakes literally hard as rock - speak to Cook.

November 3rd

Look through clothes laid out for me to choose from and decide I have *nothing* whatsoever to wear. Nothing that is, which is not ancient, out of fashion or plain dreary. Eventually Agnes dresses me in plum stripe overdress with long sleeves. Add single diamond drop on black velvet choker in vain hope it 'lifts' the ensemble. Only pray no one remembers seeing the gown before as it has had at least two previous outings. Agnes has cleverly attached black lace to the neckline and cuffs to disguise the fact. My maid is quite an asset, so talented with needle and thread. What would I do without her?

Hope never to find out.

Spencer, recovered from another night of over indulgence, looks handsome in grey silk but refuse to tell him as am still cross because he lost heavily at cards - again. Will he never learn?

Answer comes there none.

Arrive at High Brow House an hour later than everyone else. Even though I specifically asked Beloved Husband to arrange carriage to be brought around at three, he says I am mistaken and why could I not ask for it myself? Give him three good reasons two of which involve servant problem and the third concerning his Son and Heir who decided today of all days to be violently ill all over the nursery.

Journey to Dear Hattie's conducted in silence.

My sister, charming in mauve and silver which to my eye resembles storm clouds, sympathises when I tell her Spencer Jnr under the weather due to polishing off gooseberry tart stolen from the kitchen - this in addition to his luncheon. Agree with her when she suggests eight year old boys appear to have hollow legs.

Dinner as always plentiful and delicious.

Later am introduced to good looking young lady with dimples who is new to the area. Say I am sure she will soon feel at home and turn to Spencer in hope he will agree with me only to find he has disappeared.

Talk about where Miss Shaw usually resides (Thirsk), the latest style of sleeve which we both agree are not to our liking and Mansfield Park which I have yet to read but understand is very good. She asks if I have read the new novel by the 'Literary Lioness' and goes on to say the latest book is a 'real page turner' and that she 'cannot put it down' - as she does not have the book in her hand see this is an exaggeration on her part. Say after I have read Mansfield Park I will certainly look out for it. She then tells me the title which I instantly forget. In truth did not know of the other book's existence but do not tell her this in case she gets the impression I am not as well read as she appears to be.

Miss Shaw is a remarkably well informed young lady. Not sure it is at all becoming.

Dear Hattie sidles up behind me and whispers that Miss Shaw has a dowry of five thousand pounds and that she is much sought after in her home environs. Agree she is delightful addition to our set and express how I am sure she will be sought after here too, especially when it is known she is well dowered. DH smiles, then heads for the refreshments and polishes off a plate of savouries quicker than you can say porker.

Treasured Spinster Friend (Susan Simmons), wearing what can only be described as a disaster in dingiest grey, tells me Miss Shaw has taken the Lakers' old house until after Christmas and that she has it on the highest authority the lady has removed to Summerbridge Hall in pursuit of her lover. Beg to know whose authority but TSF is tight lipped and says I must believe her because her source is *never* wrong. Ask her if this font of all knowledge is the same one who two years ago spread it about the entire county that Dear Hattie was to marry a penniless but handsome second son of a mine owner? She assures me it is not but looks decidedly shifty for the rest of the evening.

William, Dear Hattie's husband (not a mine owner's son but a Duke) is genial and a charming host as always.

After dinner spot our local member of Parliament Gerald Harper. Look straight through him but nod to an old suitor who has doubled in size since first we met. Count blessings I refused him. Wait ten minutes then make my way to a small ante room that leads to William's library.

In the carriage ride home Spencer all cheerful smiles and amiable chatter. BH asks if I enjoyed myself. Say I found the house party stimulating in the extreme and add I can tell he had a pleasant time. We have put our earlier disagreement behind us as we are wont to do these days. Have found over the years it is simpler to put aside differences as Spencer is easy to forgive - most of his sins at any rate.

On arrival home good moods extinguished when Housekeeper is waiting for me with pursed lips. BH, before making himself scarce, says if it is about the staff wages to tell her they will be paid by the end of the week or the end of the month at the very latest. When I enquire how this miracle is to be brought about Spencer nibbles my neck and in one deft movement removes my diamond choker. Compromise and suggest emeralds might be pawned this time as cannot be parted from the diamond drop as it goes so well with most gowns.

Housekeeper in high dudgeon about footman named Frost or Forrest. Apparently he has been caught 'pilfering' Spencer's best cognac. Caught red handed by Blake filling hip flask from decanter in BH's study. Our head butler, something of a fixture here at Upshot Hall, takes his duties seriously - thank goodness one of the servants is on the ball. Ruminate for some time on how I too might deign to steal from my employer if they had failed to pay me for the last quarter year. Housekeeper's nostrils flare and asks what I intend to do about it. She goes on to suggest it will set a bad tone if example not made of 'pilfering' footman. Goes so far as to say she and Blake think pilfering footman should be dismissed.

Query: Can one discharge a footman, pilfering or otherwise, if he is essentially working unpaid?

Tell Housekeeper I will speak to my husband - by the look on her face this is an unsatisfactory solution. She clearly thinks me inadequate at running my own establishment. Find pleasure gained from entertaining evening completely wiped out as a result of domestic troubles.

November 4th

Cannot rouse from my bed no matter how hard I try. Ponder several thoughts pertaining to last night whilst perusing The Lady.

1) How does Dear Hattie eat so much and still never appear to put on an ounce? At five and twenty a woman's best years are behind her but not so my sister who only grows lovelier every day. DH and The Duke are as indulgent, self-absorbed and profligate as it is possible for two people to be but I love them both dearly. Especially so when I am the recipient of DH's cast-offs.

2) When do other ladies find the time to read? Clearly they do not have a house, servants, parkland, a husband and three children to care for. How does 'A Lady' find the time to pen novels when I cannot summon the time to even read one?

3) Look into whom the 'Literary Lioness' might be so can drop it seamlessly into conversation - preferably when Lady V is in earshot. Will ask Gerald. After all he is the only one in our circle who might know or even care for that matter.

Literary ignorance once again evident on my part.

November 5th

Try a little light reading but Mansfield Park is not holding my attention.

November 6th

House in uproar as Cook says something wrong with smallest range which she relies upon when we are more than twelve to dinner. For split second consider sending note asking four guests not to come but see immediately this cannot be satisfactory solution.

Speak to Housekeeper to ascertain severity of problem. Thankfully am reassured all is not lost - only wish I had known earlier as had just spent last ten minutes mentally composing letter to *all* guests telling them entire house off limits due to contagious disease - agree to curtailed menu to pacify Cook. One cannot bend over backwards far enough for the odious woman. She threatens to give notice as often as I change my bonnet. She is not even accomplished ... or French.

Dinner great success despite earlier histrionics from Cook. I thought it only fair to place myself by The Old Colonel who can always be relied upon to bore for England. Why any of us still receive him I cannot say. Made up for him by having my brother-in-law to my right. Gerald I thought to place opposite me. Having him in my eye line yet being unable to converse with him is quite tantalising.

The Old Colonel talks of hunting - pigeon, stag, fox,

anything which moves in fact. William as always, good company and am immensely thankful for the convention of turning table or I would be bored half to death by The Old Colonel. Regardless of whether I listen or not, he drones on and on. After the fish he bemoans the pheasant problem. Mishear and agree the lower classes are getting above themselves since all the bother in France. He does not notice my faux pas but squeezes my thigh and says, 'just so my good lady, just so' which has the effect of making me feel about a hundred years old.

Query: Ask Spencer if he is prone to squeezing lady's knees under the dining table - then think better of it as fear answer will not be to my liking and will undoubtedly result in a quarrel.

When the gentlemen are at their port sit beside Miss Shaw to ensure she has everything she needs. She tells me Spencer was perfect dinner companion (had thought to sit them together as I felt sure they would hit it off) and how lucky I am to be married to such a man. Agree but say dismissively that when she has one of her own she will soon see how husbands, no matter how handsome, can be as trying as one's children.

Gentlemen take an age to return and find myself inexplicably talking about political crisis with Gerald's wife Mariah. Which crisis she refers to am uncertain but need not have worried as Mariah, as usual, needs little input from me. Realise she has very determined views and not altogether sure I agree with her radical ideas. She imagines, wrongly, we can all afford to pay servants fair wages - we can barely scrape by as it is without further expense of paying 'wages above subsistence level'.

Query: Is benevolence only possible when one is well situated oneself?

When the gentlemen finally rejoin the ladies all of them, except The Old Colonel and Gerald, take to the card tables. Interesting to see Mariah and Miss Shaw also play a hand or two of whist. Can see by look on Spencer's face he is not altogether happy about this, though he rallies and pats Miss Shaw's hand from time to time to remind her of the state of play.

Leave the room to make sure light refreshments will be served in an hour. Gerald follows and steers me into the morning room and we admire the view for some time.

November 7th

Feel oddly lethargic and do not rise until luncheon.

November 8th

With monies raised from pawning emeralds pay a dozen of the most pressing creditors and buy gifts for the children including requested rag doll for Darling Daughter Clementine, an archery set for Spencer Jnr and a hobby horse for Little Charles. Feel I also deserve reward so buy large box of favourite chocolates (ostensibly for Mama but have enough self knowledge to admit she will never taste them).

Write to ask my dressmaker if I pay something on account will she deign to make a new gown for me to wear at Christmas? If the answer comes back in the negative shall have to once again call upon the generosity of Dear Hattie, which of course I am reluctant to do. Seem to be forever getting Agnes to alter DH's last season's apparel - it is most trying to the nerves and *almost* beyond one's dignity but what is to be done?

NOTHING AT ALL.

Then have marvellous idea after sampling a fine Madeira. Suggest to Spencer he visit Aged Aunt to try to squeeze funds out of her. Point out without additional resources Christmas will be a dull affair indeed. Proposal we invite her for Christmas falls on deaf ears as realise he has fallen asleep behind his broadsheet.

November 9th

Dear Hattie pays morning call wearing the most exquisite pelisse lined with sable. Pray she tires of it soon.

When I ask her does she know the name of 'Literary Lioness' who wrote Mansfield Park (never enters my head when I am with Gerald to ask him) she attaches such a look of concentration to her face I think she may be about to faint. 'No idea' she says then adds 'is not her name Anon?'

Arrive at conclusion DH's literary ignorance worse than mine.

November 10th

Still no news from dressmaker.

November 11th

Ride out with Gerald and his sister, Mrs Rose Topping, whom I have never met before. She is recently married and returned from her honeymoon abroad. She is visiting her brother from her home at Harlow Court, which by all accounts has recently enjoyed modernisation costing thousands of pounds. Only wish we could improve Upshot Hall but until Aged Aunt expires sad to say it will remain a pipedream.

Mrs Topping is pretty and petite. Her sage green riding habit is of the very latest style. I know I am going to like her very much when she tells me her brother has said how he admires me tremendously. Looking forward to attending a supper party on Wednesday given by Gerald in honour of the newlyweds.

November 12th

Hear from dressmaker to the effect she is willing to accommodate me and therefore arrange a fitting before she can change her mind. Am dismayed to find during the fitting that my measurements have altered.

November 13th

At High Brow House stand sideways on before Dear Hattie and smooth day dress from bust to hips. Ask if she thinks I look bigger. 'Bigger than what?' she asks nibbling a biscuit. 'Bigger than usual', I reply curtly. She assures me not but the tape measure does not lie.

Decline cake and biscuits for the rest of the visit.

November 14th

Decide there is nothing else for it but to embark on a reducing diet. Agnes gives me odd look when I tell her of my plan.

Dine at Lady V's. Once again am saddled with The Old Colonel. Eat far too much in order to distract self from his tedious monologue.

November 15th

Receive letter from Mama saying she intends to visit for THREE weeks over the Christmas period, news of which almost sends me into a faint.

Am perplexed on two counts; A) Christmas will already be challenging from a financial standpoint without the further expense Mama will undoubtedly incur and B) Mama will spend entire festive season picking fault with my housekeeping skills and poor management of the children whom she will see twice - once on the day of her arrival and again three weeks later on the day of her departure. Why she wants to visit Yorkshire at all is beyond reason.

Tell Spencer, who is nodding off, of impending doom. He shrugs dismissively and suggests reinstate lie about epidemic, then thinking - wrongly - he has warded off the catastrophe he goes to sleep.

Ride over to Dear Hattie's and burst into tears when I tell her news of Mama's intended visit. She says, and I cannot say how grateful I am to hear it, she has just this very morning written to Mama to invite her to stay with them for the whole of the festive season. Am much relieved as I know Mama would much rather spend time at High Brow House where the amenities are altogether superior to ours at Upshot Hall.

We sit with our feet on the fender, as is our custom when alone, drinking port. Then jumping up and startling me so much I spill my drink, DH says she can smell burning. She then stands with her back to the fire, blocking the heat, and hoicks her skirt up to warm her behind in most unladylike fashion. However, cannot remonstrate with DH - she has always felt the cold and if she is to have Mama for Christmas I can forgive her anything.

We talk about last night's dinner party at Lady V's - both agree the food was disappointing, the latest news from France - dismal - and how our younger sister Georgiana will be lucky to find a husband if she carries on behaving as she does. It has to be said the girl cannot be trusted around men, young or old. Mama has no influence over her whatsoever which is odd as both DH and I were kept on very short leashes.

Ride home pleased at another crisis averted. Think the government should put me in charge of any future conflicts as should easily be able to save England from disaster.

Buoyant mood short lived when on arriving home Housekeeper informs me small kitchen range has officially died and what am I going to do about it. Cannot survive Christmas without it so tell her to do whatever it takes to mend or replace. More expense will naturally be incurred but what can one do?

Answer comes there none.

Am also informed the ceiling in the blue room is bowing. Refrain from asking to whom. Housekeeper is not known for her sense of humour and so leave her to deal with the problem. No doubt the roof will need to be patched *again* if it ever stops raining.

Note: Inform Spencer that there will therefore be two more calls upon our purse.

November 16th

Results of reducing diet very disappointing so far. Nothing has passed my lips except soda water and biscuits. This, according to Manuel des Dames, is one method used by Lord Byron for shedding excess weight. Decide more drastic measures called for and so determine to try fasting diet where one starves oneself ALL day. Agnes flippantly suggests she locks me in my room for twenty four hours. I find her idea most unhelpful and tell her so. When she sulks for the rest of the day I ignore her; but one cannot afford to antagonise a good lady's maid. I count myself lucky to have her, not many good maids are prepared to live in such a backwater as Killinghall.

Note: Will not be copying another of Byron's habits and eating nothing but potatoes and vinegar. The very thought is enough to make one ill.

November 17th

Spend every minute of the day in bed to avoid coming into contact with food of *any* kind. All I can think of is cake with thick icing and cream. Tried reading Mansfield Park to take my mind from eating but 'A Lady' writes of nothing but food!

November 18th

Break fast on huge slice of honey cake and copious amount of cold pork and eggs followed by deep remorse at lack of self restraint. Refuse to see Dear Hattie as she is such a bad influence and will lead me astray by pressing cake, biscuits and chocolate upon me.

Query: Would liquid diet work?

November 19th

Lovely gathering at Knox Park. Gerald's family seat stands in a dramatic position and enjoys splendid views across open countryside; even in winter it looks well. Gerald's position has indeed improved since his marriage to Mariah. Her dowry has been put to good use.

Wear my ivory silk and tell self the reducing diet is at last working. Spencer, in navy blue which brings out the colour of his eyes, looks dashing. We are late going down because of it.

Mrs Topping and her husband make handsome couple. Francis Topping looks familiar but cannot place where I might have seen him before.

Dinner is a splendid, lavish affair with no expense spared. I merely pick at each course determined not to sabotage my good intentions. Luckily for me am seated next to a very nice gentleman of middle years to my left called Hugo Bright. Have heard of him of course but we have never actually met, I believe he travels a great deal. He is attentive and charming throughout dinner and distracts me from eating too much for which I am grateful.

Hugo, though a man in his early forties, still has a twinkle in his eye but is not at all like The Old Colonel who should take heed (thankfully The Old Colonel is placed at some distance from me). To my right is Gerald's older brother. Sincerely hope Gerald does not run to seed like George. Strange how two brothers can be so different but then recall Gerald and George have different mothers.

Query: If I had another child with someone other than Spencer would the offspring look so very different from my first three?

Answer: Hope never to find out.

Mrs Topping and I discuss books. She tells me she has heard that Mansfield Park may have been written by a

Miss Jane Austen. An unmarried lady writer? Whatever next!

Spencer says Mrs Topping is no great beauty but thinks her attractive in a provincial sort of way. Am astonished as she is the height of fashion (white Indian muslin edged in pale blue). Her slender silhouette and dainty feet are to be envied I tell him. BH disagrees and says she is as nothing compared to me. Am immediately on my guard; when Spencer resorts to flattery he is invariably hiding something, or someone.

Later, manage to slip away with Gerald for half an hour. Have never dared to be in his rooms before and find it both exciting and risqué to be there, needless to say both feelings heighten our pleasure.

November 20th

Spend the day feeling nauseous, dizzy and light headed. Having drunk nothing but a little wine and a small port or two at last night's soiree can only assume that drinking on an empty stomach has brought on this unpleasant sensation. Can only nibble biscuits when am not laid prone with the blinds down.

November 21st

Feel decidedly trim but again consider the benefits of a liquid reducing diet. Agnes looks nonplussed when I air this view then says, kindly, I look lovely as I am. What would I do without my faithful maid?

November 22nd

Am forced to make morning call to Spencer's Aged Aunt but not before have fortified myself with a small sherry. These visits invariably bore me to tears. Old people have limited topics of conversation - she rarely ventures into company - therefore visits to Prospect Place sorely try the nerves.

When asked to join us at Upshot Hall for Christmas, Aged Aunt, draped head to foot in black crepe and with hands thrust into a fur muff (which turns out to be old cat) tells me she doubts she will see the end of November let alone Christmas. Having removed as many garments as possible before entering Aged Aunt's morning room, still feel top lip moist and day dress sticking to spine.

Query: Why do old people feel the cold so much? Aged Aunt meanwhile wearing martyred expression and swathes of woollen shawls with Welsh blanket draped over her knees still has blue-tinged lips.

Entire conversation conducted at a yell as Aged Aunt stone deaf. Ear trumpet, companion tells me, has 'gone missing', making dialogue of any import impossible. Decide to make small talk with companion but the woman is really a very dull creature and so give up and stare at still life of limp hare dripping blood onto pewter plate. Strong smell of camphor induces further feeling of biliousness for the whole visit. Tea is brought but note absence of comestibles apart from wafer thin slices of bread and butter which am forced to consume as will have missed tea at Lady V's which is my next port of call.

As always leave Aged Aunt not altogether convinced my visit has been profitable. Swear will not pay visit EVER again without Beloved Husband. Aged Aunt is invariably charmed by him and only tolerates me.

Query: Why is this? - Am always perfectly civil to her whereas Spencer usually falls asleep after being obsequious for five minutes.

Note: Ask BH to try to secure haunch of venison from his brother's estate in time for Christmas. Feel extremely pleased with self for thinking of economical idea. Might he also spare a saddle of lamb?

Lady V is in her conservatory when I arrive at Highbourne House. As I am shown in she looks pointedly at the tiny watch pinned to her great bosom. Realise, too late, it is way beyond the time when a morning call is acceptable. Blame lateness on Aged Aunt but Lady V says she can only spare me ten minutes as she has 'an appointment'. Feel like a pariah, then look on the bright side as will have fulfilled obligation of returning her call but will not have to put up with the insufferable woman for long.

We talk about Mansfield Park which I still have not read, but am assured by Lady V am missing nothing. Casually manage to slip in a reference to the 'Literary Lioness' possibly being a lady named Miss Austen, in hope it makes me sound intelligent. Lady V scoffs and says it is 'a ridiculous idea' a lady should write a novel.

For once I agree.

Before I take my leave we go on to discuss the price of good silk brocade and the shortcomings of above stairs servants.

November 23rd

Heavy rain ALL day long.

November 24th

Ate nothing at all until dinner.

November 25th

Woke with strange hollow feeling inside. Does this mean I am losing weight?

November 26th

When Miss Grimes presented the children this evening dismayed to see Darling Daughter Clemmie's hair is rapidly losing its lustre. Gone are the blonde tresses to be replaced with locks of a decidedly mousy hue. Notice Spencer Jnr's blonde curls still adorable. This is most unfair as DDC will have only her looks to depend on as she grows up. How will she secure an advantageous marriage with lacklustre hair?

Give several minutes thought to finding a solution before asking Agnes, who is an expert in all things of this nature, for assistance. Rinsing her hair with lemon juice will do the trick she assures me. Miss Grimes looks unconvinced but I insist she try the remedy.

November 27th

Am certain I have lost weight. At last.

November 28th

When I tell Spencer Aged Aunt is to come to us for Christmas, heated discussion regarding the merits of the idea threatens marital harmony. Point out I have no particular wish to scream myself hoarse or swelter in my own home but if, as he hopes, she is to leave him her entire fortune on her demise, then sacrifices must be made. He counters saying he has 'everything in hand' then adds he had planned to go to see her on Christmas Eve with suitable impressive gift which would have been sufficient. Say forcefully had he only thought to tell me!

Irony lost on him as always when he is caught out in a lie.

Spend afternoon making lists of economies we might make to enable us not to bankrupt ourselves over festive period. Spencer adds fuel to the fire when he says from behind his newspaper that he cannot understand why I am making such a fuss as we will be at my sister's from Christmas Eve to St Stephen's day. Pointedly remind Beloved Husband Christmas festivities last twelve days and we shall be expected to entertain on at least three of those unless I can find some excuse. Thought of contagious illness beginning to look appealing.

Supper party held here at Upshot. Dear Hattie, William, Gerald, Mariah, Miss Shaw and BH's Boring Cousin Arthur in attendance. Boring Cousin Arthur and The Old Colonel should get together - am sure they will have much in common and spare us all their tedious speeches.

Spencer later complains the fare was 'poor, verging on inedible'. Point out twelve courses can hardly be described thus although wish Cook would either decide to burn the meats or undercook them; both in one sitting is confusing to the taste buds.

Spencer's criticism gives me perfect opportunity to suggest he speak to Freddie regarding venison for Christmas. BH scowls and changes subject by saying he proposes to share my bed tonight. Allow him the pleasure as thought he looked particularly handsome earlier and it is always easy to get him to think as I do when he gets his own way.

November 29th

Darling Daughter Clemmie's hair still decidedly dull. Fear she takes after me; Agnes says all too often that I have 'difficult' hair.

November 30th

Letter from Mama saying she will not be spending

Christmas with us after all as she is to spend it with Dear Hattie and her 'dear, dear husband'. What Spencer can have done to upset Mama I can only speculate. Am almost sorry for him, but not quite. Once again he lost heavily at cards last night. If only he could hit a winning streak.

December

December 1st

Suspect there is still something suspicious going on with Spencer as he continues to be solicitous - nauseatingly so. This morning, quite without warning he said I was looking 'delightfully svelte'. Perhaps his silver tongue is a way of making me look the other way. Decide to pay particular attention to his behaviour from now on.

December 2nd

A new hunter arrived at the stables this morning! I *knew* something was afoot. Ask BH how can we possibly afford this extravagance? BH replies he won the horse in a bet. Point out a pig flying by the window before storming out of the room thoroughly exasperated.

Insolvency thy name is Spencer.

December 3rd

Afternoon entertainments at Nidd Hall with Lucy and St John Smythe. Ordinarily we do not care to accept invitations from them but Gerald sent a note saying he would be there if I could 'manage to get away'. Thoughtfully Spencer had a prior engagement. After our last meeting Gerald is most eager to see me again, which I must admit, is quite flattering.

No one of interest ever attends the Smythe gatherings - St John is an outrageous, old lech. He spends all night making lewd remarks - what an embarrassment for Poor Lucy. Was once cornered by him and was obliged to ask him to let go of my person or else I would scream. On another occasion he pinched my bottom so hard I was bruised for a week. One has to feel for the wife of such a man. Shudder at the thought of sharing a bedchamber with him. Poor Lucy.

Spend all evening with Gerald trying to get St John off my tail. Finally - and this makes me smile - Mariah falls into St John's trap as Gerald and I make good our escape to a side room which thankfully has a fire lit.

December 4th

Begin reading Mansfield Park again - it is so long since I picked it up have quite forgotten how it begins.

December 5th

Dear Hattie calls wearing charming deep red day dress with matching outrageous but beautiful hat. She picks up my book and says if she has a daughter she may name her after the heroine of 'A Lady's' novel. Cannot say am enraptured by the idea of having a niece named Fanny but think it unkind to say so. Ask DH if she has any news on that front but it appears not. Strange, as The Duke looks a virile sort of man to my eye.

Pull chair nearer to fire as DH blocking heat by standing too close as usual. Reflect she would make an excellent fire guard. Maid is summoned and DH says she would not be at all disappointed to find a glass of sherry and bite to eat by her side. The Duke's food bill must be larger than the national debt. DH eats for two when she is not with child, how much will she consume when she 'falls'?

December 6th

Dear Hattie says Mama has written to say our sister Georgie has run away from school again and this time they are refusing to take her back. Both agree we expect Mama to be totally unreasonable at Christmas, even more so than usual because of this new development. Georgie too will no doubt be bad-tempered and surly. Our sister's sense of self preservation will render all others responsible for her predicament. She will be unbearable and Mama will wash her hands of her youngest daughter for the duration of the visit, meaning DH and I will be acting chaperones. This is a thankless task and one that will render all three of us insensible by the end of the first week. It will be like trying to hold onto quicksilver. Georgie can lose chaperones like I lose handkerchiefs.

December 7th

Once again am dismayed to find finances in disarray. Cannot fathom how this happens as my records are meticulous. Ask Housekeeper why grocery bill is higher than usual. Am convinced someone is swindling us. 'Lemons' she states emphatically. When I query this odd remark she tells me Miss Grimes has put in a weekly order for lemons and they have to be sent direct from Covent Garden. 'Lemons', Housekeeper goes on to inform me, are 'dearer than rubies'. Am about to remonstrate with her when remember Agne's idea to bring back shine to Darling Daughter Clemmie's hair.

Summon Head Gardener. When Brown arrives ask him if the hot house is capable of producing lemons and am told it is and it does. Am astounded! Why then are we purchasing said fruits from Covent Garden at vast expense when we have our very own trees? Resolve to have stern words with Housekeeper *and* Miss Grimes.

December 8th

Spencer bowls into the withdrawing room, grabs both my hands, lifts me off my feet then dances me around the room - explains extraordinary behaviour after we fall over small side table breaking a dish. Great Uncle Hubert (no idea who he was) has died leaving Spencer three thousand pounds! Knees almost buckle with relief that impending financial ruin has been averted.

Suggest we pay most of our creditors and especially my dressmaker and Spencer's tailor, the servants, some of the bank loan and the wine merchant. Spencer says better to pay off as much of the bank loan as possible as interest rate is crippling, the indoor servants, the head groom, my dressmaker, his tailor and the wine merchant. Agree especially about the wine merchant (overheard Blake telling Spencer about depleted reserves of port, sherry and brandy only last week). Thought of rationing wine and spirits over Christmas has been keeping me awake at night.

Celebrate windfall by ordering three new gowns, a kaleidoscope for Spencer Jnr, a puzzle for Little Charles and two adorable bonnets for Darling Daughter Clemmie. Tell Housekeeper to double previous Christmas provisions and am thrilled to hear Spencer has instructed Blake to replenish the cellar. Order gift for Dear Hattie, six pairs of silk stockings, and purchase special chocolates for Agnes. Without my maid's inventiveness with a needle and thread I would appear a drudge of the first order.

Later, Spencer and I take pleasure in each other, enjoying the one remaining bottle of champagne knowing there will be more where that came from. Sleep like a log for the first time in weeks.

December 9th

After seeing self in the looking glass this morning decide only to smile in public to avoid possibility of more wrinkles marauding over face.

December 10th

Ride out with Dear Hattie but we are forced to turn back earlier than planned when it comes on to snow. Take refuge at the nearest house which sadly belongs to The Old

Colonel. Leave after half an hour as it is colder in his withdrawing room than it is outside. It is hardly surprising he is a bachelor; no lady could live in such temperatures. Need several glasses of brandy to thaw out on regaining own home which is mercifully warm.

Note: If this encounter had been in a novel we would have been forced to take shelter at the abode of a handsome, agreeable gentleman and not shiver in a draughty withdrawing room sipping tepid tea and eating week old cake (type unknown).

December 11th

Sneezed three times in quick succession. I blame The Old Colonel.

December 12th

Remind Spencer to collect emeralds from pawn broker in Harrogate.

December 13th

Whilst on my errands bump into Miss Shaw (smart red coat with astrakhan collar and matching hat and muff). Graciously ask her to tea tomorrow. She apologises and says she is already engaged. Suggest two other dates but she cannot accommodate me on either one.

Query: Am I justified in feeling rebuffed? I have so much to do with Christmas just around the corner and only asked her out of courtesy. On walk home resolve never to importune the young lady again.

December 14th

Suddenly and inexplicably recall how I know Francis Topping.

Query: Why is it when one sets one's mind to remembering something it quite escapes detection yet the minute one forgets about it the information turns up out of the blue?

If I am not very much mistaken Francis Topping was once in the militia and was involved in a scandal with a young heiress. Is it not mortifying Gerald's sister should be married to a rake? I cannot see him turning out to be dependable or faithful. Why would Gerald allow his sister to marry such a rogue? No doubt Topping married Rose for her dowry. Remind self that this is the reason most men marry, my own BH being no exception although he is, naturally, devoted to me.

December 15th

When I tell Dear Hattie about Francis Topping she annoys me immeasurably by calling me 'a fool' and laughing so hard she almost chokes on a biscuit. She tells me that was a man called Fredrick Tiptree and that he eloped with the heiress only to leave the poor lady when he had spent all her money. Point out haughtily it was an easy mistake to make as the names are not dissimilar. She then guffaws in a most improper fashion and says, 'You are a one' which she thinks is acceptable but I do not. Leave earlier than planned feeling ridiculed at her frankness.

December 16th

Dear Hattie sends note of apology and begs forgiveness for her behaviour yesterday. As the note is accompanied by a large box of my favourite chocolates I decide to be magnanimous.

She calls and we take luncheon together before I try on the new gown the dressmaker has sent over this morning. DH says it knocks years off me and makes me look pounds lighter. I love my sister; she can always be counted on to restore my spirits.

December 17th

Overhear Spencer Jnr telling his sister that 'Blake is a lobcock'. Am so shocked I insist Spencer speak firmly to his son. When asked what Son and Heir has said tell him to enquire of Spencer Jnr himself as it would not be ladylike to repeat the utterance. BH laughs and tries to make me tell him but I am resolute and will not repeat it under any circumstances. This is not the first time I have had to have words with Miss Grimes regarding eldest son's inappropriate language. Of course cannot bring myself to repeat the word to her and so we talk at odds for some time until I can make her aware Spencer Jnr should be watched more closely especially around his impressionable younger sister. She apologises and assures me she will do her best to reprimand son but fears he takes little notice of her.

Relay this information to BH who says nothing.

December 18th

Mrs Topping makes a morning call. We talk about our respective Christmas arrangements, the merits of sable as opposed to fox and how she is tired of sitting for her portrait. It is at first exciting to have one's image painted for posterity I agree but it soon becomes boring when one is expected to stay mute and still for hours on end.

Only glad I was painted in my younger days. Imagine if an artist took it upon himself to produce too realistic an image nowadays. The thought does not bear thinking of for long.

December 19th

After hearing the nativity story from her nursemaid Darling Daughter Clemmie shows excessive interest in the concept of a Virgin birth. We are in the nursery when she asks what a virgin is and am I one? Is Miss Grimes one? Is she one and can a man also be in this state? Direct child to storyteller for answer and make hasty exit. Hear Spencer Jnr roaring with laughter and telling DDC that the story is all 'bunkum' and he should know because his father told him so after church on Sunday.

Mention to Spencer desirability of not expressing his opinions in front of easily influenced young minds, to which he shrugs and then mutters rude comment the gist of which I cannot possibly repeat.

Query: Was I so inquisitive at six years of age?

December 20th

Insufferable behaviour from Lady V this morning. Do I know she tells me, Treasured Spinster Friend has let it be known that Miss Shaw is 'not who we think she is'. She goes on to say it is scandalous that TSF has 'nothing better to do than spread malicious gossip'. This she delivers in most condescending manner - as if I have any control over TSF's shocking tittle tattle. Explain, smiling through gritted teeth, what TSF says or does is no responsibility of mine, to which Lady V humphs. Unsure how to respond to the sound so offer her tea. Lady V goes on to say, unkindly, that if TSF had a husband she would have less time on her hands for 'idle chit chat and rumour mongering'.

It is a fault in Lady V, one of many I might add, that she does not bother to cultivate the feelings of those less fortunate than herself. TSF's unmarried state, in Lady V's eyes, renders her beneath contempt and so she belittles her instead of pitying her.

Rest of visit strained not to mention tedious.

Note: Speak to Cook. To the best of my knowledge the seed cake is at least four days old and as dry as dust. Cook makes a habit of producing horrors each time Lady V visits.

Not half an hour after departure of Lady V, Treasured

Spinster Friend arrives and promptly bursts into tears just as Spencer sits down to take coffee. BH says nothing, looks accusingly at me and then takes his coffee elsewhere.

Calm TSF with small sherry and ask her what the matter is. Am informed Lady V has blamed her for spreading rumour when she has 'done no such thing'. Long rambling story then unfolds details of which I can barely follow. Top and bottom of it is, as TSF told me last month, that Miss Shaw is in the provinces in pursuit of a gentleman (name unknown) and is no better than she ought to be but TSF assures me she has not breathed a word about it to ANYONE.

Spend rest of day considering who Unknown Gentleman can be. By suppertime have produced a short list of three candidates: Beloved Husband's Boring Cousin Arthur (right age but unlikely as he is BORING), Captain Rainer recently arrived with the militia (most likely candidate as he is quite the stylish soldier in his uniform), or William's younger brother Walter (concede this last one improbable as he is not yet eighteen years of age).

Spend some time trying to decide what age Miss Shaw can be. Decide no older than twenty. If only she had agreed to come to tea, feel certain I should have been able to winkle it out of her somehow.

December 21st

Tell Spencer if he forgets to get the emeralds from the pawn broker AGAIN today they will be lost forever. Remind him three more times before he leaves the house.

Note: Nerves cannot stand the strain of anticipating loss of family jewels every few months. Vow to think of other ways to raise money in the New Year. What these ways will be I have no idea. Consider briefly if writing popular novel (perhaps about a house like Mansfield Park and heroine *not* named Fanny) would be profitable.

Spend morning writing letters and meeting with Housekeeper regarding last minute arrangements for Christmas. Remind her Aged Aunt's room to be kept hotter than Hell for duration of visit come what may.

Approach problem of last night's overdone beef. Housekeeper says she will take up the matter with Cook. Half an hour later she returns saying Cook astonished as she always thought 'the master preferred his beef well done'.

December 22nd

Note received from Aged Aunt. Says it is far too cold for her to leave her house and what was I thinking expecting a lady at her time of life to be 'gadding' about the county in December? Just as well she has changed her mind; AA would have had to venture out again to spend Christmas at High Brow House as had quite forgotten she was coming to us when I accepted DH's invitation.

Tell Housekeeper to damp down all fires and heave huge sigh of relief.

Weather dreary in the extreme. Cannot stir myself to step out of the door - or away from the fire. Decide to learn by heart a verse or two of Milton - might it not be pleasing to guests if I could recite for them? Sadly, brain is unable retain a single line so give up and play cards with Spencer instead.

December 23rd

Find myself in Beloved Husband's study. Alarmed to read letter from bank lying casually on blotter. Am incredulous to see Spencer has taken out further loan for two thousand pounds! 'Why?' I ask thin air. Resolve to ask *him* but not until after Christmas. Do not want to spend all of festive season arguing or worse still not on speaking terms.

Whilst idly perusing desk drawers find blue leather jewel box of a size and shape that would indicate a bracelet is inside. Dither for a moment deciding whether to take a peek. Wonder also why Spencer has not put what is presumably my Christmas present in the safe. Make sure study door locked then open box. Inside is an exquisite diamond bracelet. Closer inspection shows a gold 'S' charm - my initial - by the clasp. Lump comes into throat and am overcome with emotion at adorable and expensive gift. What a splendid man I married.

That night at the Pascoe's party I am especially attentive to BH - so much so I believe he suspects I am up to something.

December 24th

Christmas Eve - Spencer less helpful than I would wish and takes up typical male stance regarding packing for three days stay at High Brow House. When I ask if his man knows what to take he waves his hand dismissively and mutters something about going away for three days not three weeks, a comment I find less than supportive.

All the children's clothes along with my trunks packed, then realise not all BH's luggage will fit into the carriage. BH says, unsympathetically, that it will fit if the children walk. By the time we leave for Dear Hattie's we are no longer on speaking terms.

Wonderful Christmas party thrown for fifty of the duke and duchesses closest friends and family. Pleased to meet Hugo Bright again whom I first met at Knox Park. Once again I find him to be delightful company and a good dancer to boot. I like Hugo - he misses nothing - his sharp eye and acerbic tongue are quite compelling, especially when I realise he has the measure of Lady V who fawns and flutters over him unaware he is mocking her outrageously.

Another reason I have taken to Hugo is that over supper he tells me, in conspiratorial tone, how he thinks all forms of broadening one's outlook are a 'complete waste of time' and that books are 'the devil's work'. He laughs when I tell him my plan of self improvement then adds I am perfect as I am and cannot be improved upon. What a lovely gentleman. Pray Lady V does not get her claws into him.

Wear hair in new style copied by Agnes from latest edition of The Lady. This fashion periodical is essential reading for Dear Hattie and I who otherwise would be quite like country mice. My new style is admired by all.

New white gown (embroidered ivy and berries on the bodice) is also much admired - except by Mama of course. She says (thankfully out of earshot of the other ladies) I am a little 'long in the tooth' to wear white. Point out all court wearing white this season regardless of age. Mama sniffs and says DH and Georgie look delightful in white because they have the skin to carry it off. Decide to rise above unfair criticism and pray empire line never goes out of fashion as it hides a multitude of sins.

Sadly the evening is marred when Georgie flirts outrageously first with William and then with Spencer. Both indulge her which only makes her worse. She then sets her cap at Captain Rainer but he, sensible man, gives her no encouragement whatsoever. Yet she is shameless and undeterred. Without doubt she will be making a nuisance of herself and determined to be in love with him before the festivities are over. Mama pretends not to notice but tells all who will listen how Georgiana is *the* most accomplished of her three daughters and will make any man a wonderful wife.

Later Georgie tells me if she had the choice whether to marry Spencer or The Duke she would choose William even though Spencer is the more handsome of the two. Say pertly, as both gentlemen are already married, she will never have the choice but am curious as to her reasoning. She informs me she would choose DH's husband because A) he is a duke and B) he is rich.

Query: Why was I not this mercenary before marriage?

Expect Georgie to marry a prince at the very least. For a girl of fifteen my sister has decidedly fixed opinions. Later she also tells me if Spencer and I share the same bed 'at your age' and as we already have an heir then that is 'too ripe and ready by half'. Point out her language is once again inappropriate. Where she picks up these sayings I shudder to think.

Georgie can be very trying on the nerves. I pity any future husband.

After supper dance with William, Walter, Gerald and Captain Rainer. Interrogate them all hoping for revelation regarding Miss Shaw's Unknown Gentleman. Useful information is not forthcoming. Captain Rainer goes so far as to say he has yet to meet the lady. Does this then rule him out completely or is he being discreet? Decide to believe him. Generally I am a good judge of character and see how if he is indeed the Unknown Gentleman he would do well not to shout it from the rooftops. Is he being judicious? I hope not. I find I am quite enthralled by him. I do like a man in regimentals.

Spencer still sulking after our earlier quarrel. Do not see him for upwards of two hours. Presume him to be drowning his sorrows with The Duke's best cognac. When he does appear he whispers sweet apology in my ear and says he will make it up to me in a way that will make me believe Christmas has come early. We are not late to bed.

December 25th - Christmas Day

High Brow House. Wonderful but exhausting day. We are a select few, there being just twenty to sit down to the Christmas feast. Mama had to cover Georgie's wine glass after her third; my sister is overly fond of wine for a girl not yet presented. Pray Darling Daughter Clemmie does not take after her aunt. After more than a dozen courses where the finest food and drink is served feel ready only to sleep.

When children brought down and their presents opened, Darling Daughter Clemmie presents Mama with hand stitched sampler which she has worked herself. Such a proud moment. Dear Hattie exclaims what a clever girl she is to fill the long, awkward silence that follows. Mama inspects the stitches hoping to find errors but when none are found she sniffs and frightens the poor child half to death by kissing her cheek.

Note: Believe this to be the first time Mama has ever demonstrated affection to DDC.

Later we open our gifts, compose face to look surprised at Beloved Husband's offering of exquisite diamond bracelet. As Spencer is about to give me his present DH excitedly hands me beautifully wrapped box containing a copy of a gown I showed her in La Belle Assemblée. My sister is truly an astonishing woman. Spencer then hands me handsomely wrapped box which is far too big to be a diamond bracelet. Try to hide confusion. Unwrap gift to find pretty blue satin slippers with silver buckles. No need to feign surprise after all. Surmise he wants to give me the bracelet later, romantically, privately.

Suggest early night.

December 26th - St Stephens Day

Highbrow House. Sprinkling of snow overnight adds festive touch when we gather to see off the hunt. Stirrup cup most reviving. View hunting with detachment these days - far too dangerous a pastime for married lady with three children. Dear Hattie and The Duke look the epitome of what a handsome couple should be to my eyes. Captain Rainer looks handsome and every bit the soldier. Spencer too looks the part mounted on his trusty black steed, supposedly 'won in a bet'. Children are adorable on their ponies as they are led off by grooms.

Note: Did not have Miss Shaw down as hunt follower, just goes to show one can never tell.

Had thought to while away morning reading Mansfield Park when surprised by Gerald, whom I thought was still abed. He presents me with a beautiful belated Christmas gift. Fancy him remembering sapphires are one of my favourite stones. Show my appreciation enthusiastically.

Drinks are served when the hunt returns. Georgie, who has parted company with her mount and is covered in mud, does not join us. Agree with Captain Rainer how luncheon is particularly welcome after exercise.

Later Spencer announces it is out of the question to stay

another night as planned! When questioned he cannot provide suitable reason for this extraordinary idea so suggest he go but point out forcibly I intend to stay at High Brow House. Harsh words are exchanged on both sides culminating with Spencer *insisting* I leave with him. I am all astonishment! Then all of a sudden Spencer has a change of heart and agrees I should stay and he will return home alone.

Unfathomable!

Query: Why are husbands not like open books? Just when I am convinced I can read him he does or says something utterly surprising - and not always in an uncalculated way I might add.

Diamond bracelet has yet to make an appearance which is another unsolved riddle.

With Spencer's departure the festivities recommence. Dear Hattie's raised eyebrows her only admonishment. Determine to enjoy myself and so after dinner take pleasure in dancing. We are all quite merry. Dance mostly with dashing Captain Rainer. We talk about his part in the war, the economy and local issues. Generally these are topics which would bore me to death but Fitzroy makes any subject interesting. He has the most expressive eyes. Evening so jolly almost forget Spencer and Gerald are absent. Mariah dragged her husband away earlier to visit with her sister.

December 27th

Feel decidedly unwell and unable to eat or drink a thing.

December 28th

Upshot Hall. Dinner for two dozen friends and neighbours goes without a hitch. In fact all goes off rather well. Guests compliment me on the many and varied courses which I have to admit are more edible than the usual fare Cook serves up. Our guests, judging on previous visits, were fully expecting mediocre dinner then when it turned out to be safe to eat their delight made them over-effusive. Spencer is most sociable and gracious host. I smell a rat.

December 29th

Dear Hattie has a new carriage and four.

December 30th

We dine at The Old Colonels and are twenty, which I think is a might too tight around his table. His knee brushes mine throughout and what with Gerald stroking my thigh to my right is there any wonder I get confused and fondle The Old Colonel's knee in error? Spend rest of the evening fending off the old duffer.

Query: How is it doddery old colonel's get light of foot when a young lady is in their sights? Of course we all know the answer to this conundrum.

The Old Colonel's house is as cold and draughty as a mausoleum. Think how glad I am there are too many guests as at least we can huddle together for warmth. Of course there is no dancing as The Old Colonel had thought we would not want to dance! See Gerald try to 'lose' Mariah several times but as she appears to be turning blue she clings to him like a child to a favourite blanket. The only entertainment is provided by the colonel's guests.

December 31st

Take to bed with the most horrendous cold.

January

January 1st

Am struck how a simple cold can render one so unattractive. Complexion, hair and especially nose all adversely affected. I appear to have aged twenty years overnight. However, there is one upside to being incapacitated; having lost sense of taste am positive will soon see something resembling a waistline. Effect of course will be lost when don empire line. Hope waisted gowns make a comeback for spring.

Note: Make New Year Resolution to read more widely.

January 2nd

Lady V sends over odd looking potted plant with note expressing good wishes for my speedy recovery. Surely exotic fruit from her hothouse would have been more apt gift.

Thank God for Dear Hattie who is excellent nurse and ensures I have adequate supplies of brandy and chocolates which is well known cure for colds. She also leaves a velvet bag containing enough coin to pay the butcher, the grocer, and also the coachman.

Query: Why does one always feel safer when coachman fully recompensed?

Answer: Because fear he might be otherwise tempted to run us off the road and leave us for dead.

Treasured Spinster Friend sits on the side of my bed eating *my* chocolates and drinking *my* brandy. Says she knows exactly how I feel because she had a most *terrible* cold all over Christmas, much worse than the one I am suffering. In fact she points out my ailment is but a sniffle in comparison. Says her cold was made all the worse as she had lumps in her throat the size of hen's eggs making swallowing impossible. Do not possess enough energy to point out this not feasible or else she would be DEAD.

Begin to think of death as blessed relief from this misery.

Query: Would I get away with murdering TSF whilst the balance of my mind was affected due to raging fever?

January 3rd

Can only idly peruse The Lady.

January 4th

Still knocking at death's door.

January 5th

Spencer puts his head around my bedchamber door for first time in days and tells me he has had a sore throat for *weeks* but would not dream of making a fuss and have I seen his silver topped walking cane, the one with the lion head?

January 6th

Still feeling weak but have managed to force down a little food. Little by little brandy is helping to ease throat which does not feel as if I am swallowing glass anymore.

January 7th

Manage to partake of a light broth which I find oddly comforting. Also manage soft boiled quail's eggs and a spoonful or two of calf's foot jelly. Still look a fright so decide to keep to my rooms. Agnes is quite a proficient card player. Am dismayed to lose three shillings in the course of the afternoon.

January 8th

Manage, with Agnes's help, to take a warm bath. Spencer arrives (inconveniently) just as I am stepping out of the tub and says I am too thin. He manages to say this with much censure! As if I can help it. At times my husband can be quite trying.

January 9th

First day out of bed. Still feel like a damp dish rag. (No idea what one is but am quoting Agnes whose favourite saying it is when she feels under the weather.) Spend all day on chaise longue in front of a blazing fire drinking brandy laced chocolate and sending to kitchen for morsels to tempt me to eat.

Do not feel up to visit from Darling Children when it is suggested by Miss Grimes. The girl is dim-witted for certain. I could still be contagious.

January 10th

Tell Pilfering Footman (Frost/Forrest), who am surprised to find still in evidence, I am not at home to callers of any description. Half an hour later Lady V is shown in. When I am stronger will tell Housekeeper to let Pilfering Frost (or Forrest) go without a reference. Cannot help but feel his attitude is altogether unsuited to this establishment and had I felt well enough would have told him so in no uncertain terms.

Partake of excellent cognac for medicinal purposes.

January 11th

Lose all track of time.

January 12th

Lady V calls AGAIN. Says did I know the best thing for a cold is to put one's head over large bowl of steaming hot water to which menthol concoction has been added. Tell her have heard of the cure and will be sure to try it - another lie.

Cannot help but feel Lady V has only come to gloat over my incapacity and to see Spencer. As BH not been spotted for days she is out of luck.

Before taking her leave Lady V says she will be visiting the spa in Harrogate for a few days and would I like to accompany her? Spa will do me the *world* of good she assures me as she looks me up and down. Feel relapse coming on as try, unsuccessfully, to convey I am not up to leaving the house let alone being away from home.

January 13th

At last feel marginally better.

January 14th

Reunited with Dear Children who are even louder and more boisterous than usual. Spencer Jnr says he was sure I was about to die and orphan him. What a vivid imagination the child has!

January 15th

Rejoin the land of the living. Agnes sets her mind to restoring vitality to my lifeless hair but feel it will take more than eggs and lanolin to restore it. I fear my 'difficult hair' has lost what little bounce it had. It resolutely refuses to curl and so am forced to sleep in cloth curlers.

January 16th

Still tired and listless but am determined to soldier on.

January 17th

Agnes spends hours trying to make me look presentable. Pallid is not a good look on any lady. Dark shadows beneath my eyes and a dull, blotchy complexion are decidedly unbecoming.

January 18th

Hair still refusing to behave so instruct Agnes to pull hair back into a chignon and attempt curls only about my face. Agnes suggests a turban but in the end we opt for a head-dress composed of ivory gauze confined with a band of pearls. Again I give thanks for my maid's inventiveness.

Spencer has to be roused at five in the afternoon in order to be ready to welcome our guests for tonight's revelries. After losing heavily at cards he predictably stayed up all night drowning his sorrows. BH suffering the after effects of over indulgence very trying when attempting to arrange seating plan; he objects to everyone I place next to him. He only rallies when Freddie arrives.

Brother-in-law as usual is all smiles and good humour - what an attractive man he is. How different life would have been had I been fortunate enough to marry the elder son and not the impoverished second. After supper he takes me into the library and asks 'how is everything?' which we both know is code for 'how much in debt is Spencer?' He lets out a long whistle when I declare half the amount so Lord knows what he would say if he knew the full extent of our obligations.

Almost fall at his feet when he says to send largest bills to him and he will 'sort them out'. It is best Spencer is not told of our arrangement BIL says and I understand his reasoning perfectly. Spencer has never been good with money (or anything else really) except for spending it or losing it at the card table or the races of course.

Freddie's pretty, plump wife Gwendolyn, pink lace frothing everywhere and far too much in evidence - the lace not Gwen - says when eldest daughter is to be finished she is considering chaperoning her. I would think she would stay by Freddie's side as there is still no male heir to be seen. It is possible that at two and thirty her time has passed but is it not a wife's duty to keep trying? (Especially so as Freddie is handsome, good natured, and not to mention rich.)

Note: Should I encourage Gwen to go to Switzerland? If a male heir not forthcoming surely it puts Spencer in a much better position.

January 19th

Words cannot express how good it is to feel fresh air on one's face as I venture out on little shopping trip. Visit dressmaker to have two gowns altered. Now I have new slender silhouette my clothes positively swamp me - one bonus from being in extremis at least.

January 20th

Before breaking my fast write to Old London Acquaintance who has house in Grosvenor Square in vain hope of an invitation.

A mild, sunny winter's day which cheers and makes one believe that with luck Lady V will be out so call at

Highbourne House. As if to be contrary she is in residence. Find her arranging flowers of every gaudy colour one can imagine. Tell her she is so talented and if only I had the skill or indeed the blooms. Lady V insists I take a basket of flowers back to Upshot Hall. I thank her profusely. What a pity I 'lose' them on the way home. Lady V more generously offers hot chocolate - infused with long pepper, cardamom and cinnamon - so the visit not totally wasted.

Note: Addition of brandy to the recipe would surely enhance the taste further - must try it as soon as possible.

We talk about The Duchess of Lancaster's new carriage, Lord Coniston's recent good fortune and whether it will snow later. We agree it probably will.

January 21ˢᵗ

Bump into Miss Shaw out walking - am surprised she is still in the vicinity as was given to understand she had returned to Thirsk. Speculate, not for the first time, if any of Treasured Spinster Friend's intelligence is sound? Pointedly do not ask Miss Shaw to Upshot Hall but then feel mortified when she invites me to take tea tomorrow. Say quickly, 'Oh how lovely I was about to extend an invitation to you'.

Query: Am I right in thinking lies are not really a sin if they save one from hurting another person's feelings? As when I say Gwen looks well in ruffles and lace when in fact she looks like a cream puff.

January 22nd

Am shown into elegant south facing sitting room where Miss Shaw and her companion are awaiting my arrival. Miss Shaw says I am good to come and see her and what a beautiful shade of watercress green I am wearing. Might a revision of my opinion regarding Miss Shaw's character be necessary?

Whilst getting ready earlier I chose three other gowns before finally plumping for this one. Am gratified I appear to have made the right choice for once. Last night Spencer asked was I planning on wearing *that* just as we were about to step into the carriage. When asked what was wrong with my gown he replied 'nothing, get in the carriage before you start complaining you are cold'. The rest of the evening was indeed cold as was my shoulder when I turned it to him at bedtime.

Miss Shaw serves excellent tea. As always wonder at how everyone else is able to summon delicious savouries and scrumptious tasting cakes without any effort whatsoever. She hands me my tea in a delicate porcelain tea cup decorated with snowdrops which she tells me are her favourite flower. At once notice exquisite diamond bracelet very like the one Spencer had in his desk drawer. Mind temporarily goes blank as she asks me to help myself to sugar. As she hands the tongs notice small gold initial 'S' charm by clasp ... Please call me Serena Miss Shaw begs. She thinks we have known each other *too* long not to be on first name terms. We talk about the latest books, how lucky we are to have springs rich in both sulphur and iron practically on our doorstep and how she has changed her plans and has now decided to extend her stay until early summer.

Later, find myself in Spencer's study with the door locked. Empty every drawer but exquisite diamond bracelet with gold 'S' charm by the clasp is missing. Check safe - twice.

In my dressing room say casually to Beloved Husband I intend to wear my cream tonight as the diamond drop goes so well with it. Add what a pity it is I do not have a diamond bracelet to match. Watch BH closely but his face is innocence personified. He suggests I wear the burgundy. Kisses my neck and glances at me with the look he reserves for when he is in the mood to be amorous. Ignore him and ask caustically does he mean the gown I wore a few nights ago which he so disparaged?

He is surprisingly light on his feet for a tall man and dodges as I fling a silver hairbrush at him. He then asks what in God's name is wrong with me. I am far too heated to explain of course and so the rest of the evening is somewhat strained.

January 23rd

Still fuming over mystery of exquisite diamond bracelet with gold 'S' charm by the clasp. Conclude there is no ambiguity. Am even more furious.

January 24th

Spend morning at my correspondence. Can never think of anything interesting to tell Mama no matter how long I sit and stare at the empty page. At last tell her how much I enjoyed seeing her and Georgiana at Dear Hattie's over the festive season. Another untruth -spend all my life telling falsehoods to one person or another.

Why is this?

Note: Ask Dear Hattie if, in her opinion, this makes me a bad person - the vicar would possibly say it does. Decide DH is better placed to answer this query as the vicar does not live in the *real* world and anyway would probably read me a sermon.

Housekeeper brings menus for the week and am forced to tell her *again* we do not care for rich sauces with every course. This matter is becoming a weekly occurrence.

January 25th

Spend happy morning *indisposed* with The Lady. Beautiful fashion plates espousing what we should be wearing this spring (if only I could afford them). Instruct Cook to prepare hot chocolate a' la Lady V. When it is brought I add a dash or two of brandy and am thrilled at the result.

Note: Remember to share the recipe with DH.

January 26th

Aged Aunt arrives but refuses to get out of carriage and come into the house. Stand outside in the freezing wind while she shouts through the window. She tells me it is far too cold to be out in 'this weather'. Reason for this extraordinary visit unclear but companion (through open window which Aged Aunt tells her to close immediately), says they were on their way to visit 'A Friend' but the weather is unfit for someone of Aged Aunt's constitution and so they are returning to Prospect Place.

Once back indoors in need of reviving - take another hot chocolate with spirituous addition.

January 27th

On the fourth Sunday of every month after church we feed the vicar, his stout wife and several of their older progeny. It is a dull affair but a tradition which has been performed at Upshot Hall for centuries. No doubt when the custom was first introduced my husband's ancestors could afford to feed five extra hungry mouths. Whilst we have an impressive pedigree sadly in these times we have empty purses and so it is more of an encumbrance than I can say. Each visit it is as if they have never eaten yet I know for certain Dear Hattie and William perform the same ritual every third Sunday of the month and Gerald and Mariah every second. Even Lady V does her share on the first Sunday.

The vicar's wife is perpetually with child and so tells me she is 'eating for two'. Fear the vicar is also in this condition as he polishes off more food than I do in a week. The couple and their three eldest daughters have to be practically ejected from the house after four hours.

As usual Spencer missing for the duration of the meal which is most trying. In future will absent myself if he refuses to take his responsibility seriously, though of course know this is an idle threat. At the very least will invite more entertaining company to dilute the sermonising.

January 28th

Spend afternoon planning new wardrobe I will need for anticipated visit to London.

January 29th

Receive letter from Old London Acquaintance saying she would love to see us but will be 'sur le continent' for the entire spring and summer but perhaps they could visit us in the autumn?

January 30th

Spend much of the evening talking to Spencer about how other people are able to travel much more often than we do. Cannot remember the last time we went anywhere outside Yorkshire. He says, optimistically, that he has 'irons in the fire' which will hopefully mean we can go to London in the autumn. When pressed BH cannot promise a trip to the capital but states there is a 'high probability it will come off' - will believe it when I see it.

January 31st

Dear Hattie invites me to Harrogate so I might regain my strength by taking the waters. Suspect she is once more attempting to increase her chances of conceiving as she insists we visit Tewit which is a chalybeate well and therefore notably rich in iron. Harrogate has long been England's premier spa (yet Mama says it is *nothing* compared to Bath), the mineral waters are efficacious and the society entertaining. As a watering place Harrogate is both diverting and good for one's health, a thing that cannot be said of every town. If Mama is to be believed London is 'the Devil's playground'. One wonders if this is the case why she spends so many months of the year there.

The Duke has an elegant townhouse in Harrogate, Moorlands, overlooking the Stray so put it to Spencer the trip will incur no expense on our part whatsoever. He says nothing for a moment then says I must do as I like and that possibly I will gain some benefit from the trip but fails to see how drinking *water* can do anyone any good. And as for bathing in sulphur - BH shudders at the thought. Spencer says he will miss me, then immediately negates sentiment by asking if I will ensure Cook is made aware he will entertain whilst I am gone.

February

February 1ˢᵗ

Spend happy day deciding which clothes to take. Although we live but a short distance from Harrogate it is still exciting after being confined for so long with the plague to be going into society again. We will almost certainly meet interesting Artistic Types when we attend the Low Harrogate assembly and the Promenade Rooms to enjoy the musical recitals, dances and lectures. These will of course broaden my horizons and provide interesting or amusing nuggets to drop into conversation when I return to Upshot Hall.

Query: Would I be cleverer if I lived in Harrogate and was subjected to more elevated way of life?

Answer: I rather think I would.

Agnes again applies lanolin and eggs to my 'difficult hair' and the results are quite encouraging when a head-dress of flowers and feathers are added.

February 2ⁿᵈ

Dear Hattie calls for me at eleven. It is but a short, comfortable journey to Harrogate in her new, well sprung carriage. We chat all the way and she fills me in on all the gossip in case I missed any whilst under the weather.

Query: Is one 'over the weather' when one is recovered? The English language is a strange animal I think.

It appears I have missed that Treasured Spinster Friend was seen in Killinghall with Unknown Gentleman but unfortunately Dear Hattie was too far away to say who he might be. She says he was of medium height and build but adds she was unable to discern the colour of his hair. Speculate for some time who the gentleman could be but without more information cannot think of anyone. He cannot be a suitor I say decidedly as TSF is such a dowdy old thing these days.

February 3rd

Moorlands. Feel a thrill of excitement at the thought of meeting new people. Am always keen to broaden my mind since being forced to leave the ladies seminary earlier than I would have liked. I feel my education lacking a little because of it. I feel 'unscholarly' as it were, though Dear Hattie assures me I am every bit as learned as her and she did manage to stay the course despite several narrow escapes - was it my fault I proved irresistible to a 'gentleman' and was sent home in disgrace?

February 4th

Dear Hattie and I dine at a magnificent mansion belonging to the Earl of Scarborough. (I wear my bronze and wish emeralds were not languishing at pawn broker a dozen streets away.)

Charmed to find Hugo Bright is amongst the guests. DH makes the observation that for a gentleman in his middle years he is attractive both in appearance and in his demeanour. Agree with her completely; he always has a twinkle in his eye and a witty turn of phrase at the ready. Hugo knows how to please and always tailors his behaviour to suit each situation. He is both charming and agreeable.

The Earl has recently come into his money and has had the house redecorated in the latest style. Smart footmen circulate silently on deep pile carpets beneath glittering chandeliers. Chairs and sofas all upholstered in peacock blue silk which look beautiful but would not be comfortable to sit on for longer than ten minutes. Wallpaper and paint all very bright and cheerful. Particularly like the yellow. Would the withdrawing room at home be warmed by addition of similar shade?

Notice how many of the young gentlemen are wearing London fashions. Think how smart Spencer would look in new style attire but then think not to mention to him as cost of his wardrobe already exceeds mine. Aforementioned young bucks, many of them Artistic Types, all rather good looking. Fortunate enough to be placed at dinner next to young man wearing very modern coat. Tells me he is a poet and would not be at all surprised if he was moved to write something poetic about me. Am flattered beyond words but affect bored countenance so as not to encourage him.

Artistic Types, I know from past experience, are apt to fall in love at the drop of a hat.

Later another handsome young gentleman approaches me; suspect he has mistaken me for someone else. Says what a change to be at a lively party and don't I find most parties tiresome. Agree that I do, although this is blatant lie. He goes on to ask if I have read a book - cannot for the life of me remember title - by an author I have never heard of.

Talk generally about books and poetry and dredge memory for suitable intelligent comments - realise if only had finished Mansfield Park I might at least make a contribution which does not sound trite. As so often am struck by eloquence of other people. So glad I determined to make this the year when I read more widely. I might even attempt to read Lord Byron when I have finished Mansfield Park.

Ponder what it would be like to be immortalised in a poem.

Before bed take up Mansfield Park but fall asleep instantly. I think this proves the waters are doing me good.

February 5th

Ride out on the Stray and meet with many interesting people. Dear Hattie has a wide acquaintance here in Harrogate most of whom are extremely handsome and debonair. Afternoon entertainments overrun so much we almost miss dinner.

February 6th

Dear Hattie and I go for fittings at tre's chic modiste on Regent Parade. After seeing the latest styles displayed about the Montpelier Quarter we are determined to update our wardrobes; it is only proper we should not just follow trends but every now and then set them.

Harrogate continues to be diverting; morning calls, luncheon dates, dinners, dancing and supper parties all prove exceptionally agreeable. We crave activity and every night fall into bed exhausted.

February 7th

Together Dear Hattie and I go to a talk entitled, 'My Travels in Italy.' The speaker, a rotund little man named Mr Frank Howard, was most engaging and full of interesting little snippets about how he experienced the culture of this exciting country. He talked about the people (fiery), the food (largely comprising of something called pasta) and the climate (pleasantly warm in spring and debilitating heat in summer). The country, he tells us, boasts mountains that are snow capped in winter and lakes every bit as splendid as those in our own Lake District.

However, DH and I had not expected the talk to be quite so long and the room being full it soon became unbearably stuffy. After two hours I could feel my head nodding and my eyes closing. Thankfully at intervals DH pinched my arm or else I would have been sound asleep. Someone should tell Mr Howard that less can often be more. Despite this both

DH and I are determined to visit Italy in the near future.

February 8th

Purchase spectacular head-dress which will look just right at a spring outing. When I put it on DH says it looks like a swan has landed on my head. She is joking.

Note: Have bruises caused by DH nipping my arm at yesterday's talk. How I suffer to become well informed.

February 9th

Dear Hattie purchases two exquisite robes de chambre from exclusive establishment on Duchy Road, not even requesting the price before asking for them to be sent to Moorlands. How I wish I was able to spend money without a second thought. Treat myself to new silk stockings to cheer self up.

February 10th

Bump into Handsome Poet at St John's well. Tells me he has indeed written a poem about me and would I like to hear it? He recites poem (which does not rhyme) and I look suitably flattered even though it makes no sense as it is about a flower - how will anyone know I have been immortalised in a poem if he does not mention me by name?

Conclude Artistic Types quite odd people. Ask if he has had anything published. Tells me he is doubtful he will publish for the 'works are deeply personal'. Pity others do not take up such stance - the last book I read not worth the time and effort in my opinion. Handsome Poet tells me poem inspired by myself is titled Serena. Point out that is not my name.

February 11th

Invited to Duchess of Lancaster's elegant town house for supper party. What an evening! No expense spared and the most interesting Artistic Types and latest fashions much in evidence.

Hugo and I dance until we are much fatigued; such a lively quartet playing all the latest tunes. We are, as my sister Georgie is fond of saying, 'fagged to death' and soon in desperate need of a drink. It is a crush to get to the refreshment room but once there we find a quiet table away from the crowd. I fan myself vigorously in the hope of regaining my composure. Hugo asks what will I write about in my journal later, asks whether he will make an appearance in it - had told him previously I keep a diary - sweet of him to remember. I laugh and say I am far too discreet to mention any gentlemen by name in my scribblings - if only he knew the half of it.

When I tell Hugo that Handsome Poet has been moved to write a poem about me he laughs (somewhat derisively in my opinion). Says he will write about me 'chapter and verse' and will be sure to make it rhyme. How we laugh. He will, he says, even call it by my name so that all will know who it is about. We chortle so loudly the Duchess of Lancaster glares over and waves her fan at us admonishingly which only makes Hugo guffaw more. Fear we will never be asked back again but if it is our last visit then it has been a thoroughly entertaining evening.

Note: Had wanted D of L to be pleased with me but fear I did not succeed at all. At first I could not understand why this could be but then a thought struck me; she has a quite determined view of who she will allow into her inner circle. Clearly she only admits those who do not shine too brightly. Notice she always surrounds herself with an assortment of high ranking ladies but all of them are plain verging on drab. See how Dear Hattie and I do not fit into her criteria as we are both far too attractive.

February 12th

Letter arrives from Spencer asking why in God's name footman named Frost/ Forrest has been let go and where on earth did I think we were going to get another to work unpaid?

See how Beloved Husband will never be a poet.

Regale Dear Hattie with domestic troubles. She suggests we call at the agency to see if new footman can be recruited. Manager of high class establishment tells me I will be lucky to secure a tweeny for pay I am offering. Suggests I increase salary and when I do, reluctantly, says man named Frost available. When I demur he suggests younger, less experienced man named Snow might suit.

Do all footmen take on names of weather conditions? If so would prefer one called Fine or Fair. Decide to employ

Snow who on inspection has excellent references. As afterthought enquire about reference for footman named Frost and am told he has glowing report. From whom one can only conjecture?

Write to Spencer asking him to tell Housekeeper to expect new footman.

Note: Ascertain if indeed it is she who has written Pilfering Footman a reference when I return home. Would not put it past the man to write his own recommendation. Possibly stole note paper for the very purpose whilst drinking *my* sherry. He definitely had that look about him.

February 13th

Discuss with Dear Hattie the idea of hiring a governess for Darling Daughter Clemmie, only when funds are more stable of course. She agrees it is a wise scheme but warns not to hire a 'foreigner'. When we were children our governess was Hanoverian and very strict. Even today we cannot drink Moselle without flinching. She was eventually replaced by an excellent English governess but not before she had scarred DH and I irrevocably.

February 14th

Attend dance at which I see several acquaintances whose names I cannot remember. Spot Lady V at a distance and childishly dodge behind large potted plant where Handsome Poet asks me to dance. We dance three times. Sadly his dancing is almost as bad as his poetry. Tells me he bathes every day at the Stinking Well as he finds it 'stimulating'- that likely explains his poetry *and* his lack of prowess on the dance floor. Despatch Handsome Poet to find wine but then Lady V makes a beeline to where I am loitering hoping she has lost sight of me - sadly she has not. She is the cross I must bear.

Immediately she gushes how brave I am to venture out as she can see how I am not yet fully recovered. She assures me I look quite drawn. Lady V asks if I know excellent cure for putting spring back in one's step is bathing in the sulphur well. Am, like most right thinking ladies, horrified at the idea. How can public bathing possibly be beneficial? The very thought of Lady V venturing into the waters puts a bizarre image in one's head. Thankfully DH saves me from impolite scathing response by changing the subject.

Sister and I then partake freely of excellent wine for the rest of the evening. At least Handsome Poet has good sense of direction and finds me in the library when DH falls asleep.

Deter him from reciting by unconventional means.

February 15th

Glance in the mirror and am appalled at what I see staring back. Even Agnes knits her brows together and shakes her head. Feel all good work drinking mineral water has come to naught. Agnes spends much time trying, hopelessly, to make me appear fresh faced and not drawn. Fear loose skin beneath the eyes not becoming in a lady. Decide to cheer self up by buying another new hat.

Visit several milliners and at last see just the thing I have been searching for. Almost faint at the price (which has to be applied for) but then Dear Hattie says she will buy it for me as a gift. She laughs merrily as she charges it to her account - so glad one of us does not have to worry about money. Forego the spa waters and treat ourselves to hot chocolate and buttered toast instead.

February 16th

There are indeed some very attractive men in Harrogate and most are well bred and some 'swimming in lard' as Dear Hattie is fond of saying. Wonder idly whether any of the well off gentlemen would make suitable husband for Georgiana. Sadly, soon come to the conclusion none worth having will marry cheaply (Earl of Scarborough is quite a catch but will no doubt have his sights set on an heiress with a good dowry). Decide instead to look and admire as one would with a fine painting.

Note: Invite the Duchess of Lancaster to Upshot very soon.

February 17th

Upshot Hall. New footman has arrived and helps me from Dear Hattie's carriage wearing livery that was clearly made for much larger man.

Note: Next time we are flush will order brand new uniforms for all indoor servants. This will reflect well upon us when important guests arrive so is not an extravagance but a necessity.

Go to night nursery to see Dear Children who rush from their beds and hug me enthusiastically. Am touched by welcome. In unison all three enquire whether I have brought them a present.

Query: Was I as acquisitive as a child?

Answer: I rather think not.

At dinner, which Beloved Husband and I take alone - cannot recall the last time this occurred - Spencer says he did not like to mention before because he wanted to save me from worry but we need to make *further* economies. Mutters something about small losses at the gaming tables, then more distinctly mentions my dressmaker's bill and something he refers to as my 'little extravagances'. Say I have noted two out of the three reasons given for our indebtedness involve *my* behaviours. Ask exactly how much his *small* loses amount to and does he expect me to walk about naked? Point out I have to have clothes but he need not gamble, especially if he is going to lose.

Anticipated romantic reunion not forthcoming.

February 18th

Spencer behaving badly; his sulking is so trying on the nerves.

February 19th

Lady V calls and asks if I saw the new play at the theatre whilst in Harrogate. I say no. She asks if I partook of bathing in Stinking Well. Is the woman mad? Of course I did not. She enquires what I thought of the Dutch exhibition - which I did not attend but say it was marvellous and tell her what for me were the highlights. Handsome Poet had of course seen it and regaled me about it at length so felt like I had attended. Wax lyrical for some minutes then wish she would go so am not driven to tell even more lies.

When the repellent woman leaves, seek out Spencer who is laid prone with The Times covering his face and body, and ask if he thinks I am a bad person for telling lies? He lifts the newspaper and asks if I have lied to him. I say no of course not, what a preposterous idea. He silently replaces newspaper which I take is the end of the exchange.

February 20th

Account book refuses to balance.

February 21st

Try to embroider a pillow case but find it almost sends me to sleep after ten minutes. Take up book of poetry but it too fails to stimulate. Spend the rest of the afternoon veering between apathetic lethargy and conscious abject boredom.

February 22nd

Bills from exclusive modiste in Harrogate arrive. Feel in

need of reviving thereafter.

February 23rd

Tinker on the pianoforte for a while. I do not practise half as much as I should. If I did am sure I would be as capable as Dear Hattie who is quite accomplished.

February 24th

Poor Lucy Smythe pays me a call. After discussing my stay in Harrogate I get the distinct impression she wants to unburden herself. Cannot help but think the role of *confidante* is an apt one for me as am the soul of discretion.

She does not exactly say so, but gather from her tone she is having a *liaison* of her own - well known fact her despicable husband carries on with the *servants* so one can hardly blame her. With whom Poor Lucy is trysting have yet to find out. She is remarkably tight lipped about the gentleman concerned. Dear Hattie will know I expect. Never before has Poor Lucy paid me a call without her husband. Would gladly receive her more often if only she would leave St John at home. When first we met I thought him just an agreeable flirt; soon saw I was gravely mistaken. The man is nothing but a lecherous rogue.

Decide I like Poor Lucy in spite of her husband. When she is away from him she is a pleasant and entertaining guest and quite pretty in an unsophisticated sort of way. She has a tendency, much like Treasured Spinster Friend and Gwendolyn, to lean towards the over trimming of her gowns which to my mind is rather dated.

Poor Lucy tells me she is a great reader and I say how splendid we have this in common as I too like a good book. When I tell her about my reading list she becomes quite animated. She mentions several novels she has recently 'devoured'.

Casually ask what does Poor Lucy think about Sense and Sensibility being written by 'A Lady'. She smiles knowingly and tells me she has it on good authority the lady is a spinster from Hampshire - or is it Hertfordshire? Seem to recall Mrs Topping mentioning this titbit too. Sense and Sensibility she says is written by the same 'Literary Lioness' as Mansfield Park. If it is the same author then the lady has indeed cornered the market in fashionable book writing.

Think briefly of Treasured Spinster Friend penning a novel ... what on earth would she have to write about?

How my neighbours come upon such information is beyond me. I seem only to get knowledge at second or even third hand which is most provoking. Would like just once to be the bearer of fresh gossip or news - would it be too much to ask?

When I say I have yet to read the novels she mentions, Poor Lucy offers to send them over so I might discuss them with her when next we meet. How quaint.

February 25th

Tiresome weeks of economies brought to an end when Spencer declares a state of solvency as dividends on financial investment have exceeded all expectations. Am giddy with happiness as Spencer is not generally known for his business acumen. Never since the early years of our marriage have we been so well off. Long may this state of affairs last.

Order new peacock blue livery with gold embellishments for footmen and new afternoon uniforms for all above stairs maids. Also place order for two superior dresses for Agnes who deserves them more than anyone. What would I have done in Harrogate without her? She altered not one but two of Dear Hattie's cast offs in no time at all and without fuss or complaint. She is a jewel.

Spend the day making lists of breakages that can now be replaced and purchase pretty porcelain tea service with yellow narcissi decoration. Consider ordering yellow paint for withdrawing room but then think about disruption to household if decorators are brought in. Abandon idea until next year.

Spencer has been celebrating his business success and takes his brother to York Races. Even his losses cannot dim our sunny mood.

February 26th

Now that funds are available discuss again with Dear Hattie the idea of hiring a governess for Darling Daughter Clemmie. Together we pen an advertisement to appear in The Lady. Decide at last moment to say foreigners need not apply despite both agreeing a French governess would be preferable. Settle on the plan that English governess will be more suitable as remember our last visit to France almost ruined when Spencer took quite a liking to a Parisian countess.

February 27th

Mem: Arrange visit to Old Governess for tips on hiring lady for DDC.

February 28th

Pay visit to Miss Step our Old Governess. A fruitful and entertaining morning. Miss Step, as always, good company despite her reduced circumstances. She has many useful (and quite modern) ideas about how to secure suitable governess for Darling Daughter Clemmie. OG was always forward thinking. Could she be the reason why my sister and I turned out so well? I like to think so. After Papa died Mama had very little influence over us. She was seldom at home and when she was she spent her time making connections, rather than spending time with us.

Over tea Miss Step shows me a scrapbook which we made just before I went away to the ladies seminary. How I remember the fun we had collecting the little verses and conundrums therein - see there is even one supplied by Gerald Harper. Had quite forgotten how I had once set my cap at him. This of course was before Mama pointed out it would mean 'marrying down' - this even though he was descended from a good and ancient family - it was not however, as good and ancient as ours and so the attachment was not pursued. Happily we still have great regard for one another.

Spend an entire morning reminiscing about happy times when I was a young girl and before I married my Spencer. What fun was had at the dances and assemblies; what gowns I wore, how I was praised as a beauty. Looking back my days as a single lady were carefree and frivolous in the extreme but I would not have them back for all the tea in China. As Darling Daughter Clemmie will find to her cost, being a single lady is fraught with danger. One wrong turn and a glittering future can be ruined. It was ever thus for the fairer sex. Will do all in my power to steer DDC in the right direction. An early marriage will benefit all methinks.

It was a shame Miss Step was taken advantage of by Papa's head groom. When she was let go Dear Hattie and I cried for hours.

On my return to Upshot Hall spend cheerful hour in the music room at the pianoforte with DDC who I do believe has a musical ear. Reflect, not for the first time, how *my* love of music is all down to our Old Governess.

Whom I choose to be governess to DDC is of paramount importance I realise if, that is, she is to acquire those little accomplishments which will lift her above the mediocre and secure her a good marriage. The responsibility is not lost on me.

March

March 1ˢᵗ

Huge pile of books arrive. Poor Lucy Smythe has been kind enough to send them over. Attached is a note urging me to read one in particular as it is 'most amusing'. The book to which she refers is Mansfield Park.

March 2ⁿᵈ

Pick up Mansfield Park determined to read at least another chapter but the weather is so mild and bright give up after only a few pages. Think not to waste time indoors and take a turn about the spring garden which is just bursting into life.

March 3ʳᵈ

Instead of morning calls slip away to meet Captain Rainer. Thoughtfully Fitzroy presents me with a gift of a sable fur collar which is just the thing on a cool ride.

March 4ᵗʰ

Spencer acting in quite an odd manner.

March 5th

Darling Daughter Clemmie tells me she would like a puppy. Tell Spencer who says nothing. Realise chance of DDC getting a pet dog are remote.

Call on Dear Hattie and tell her of DDC's request. She squeals with delight and says what an amazing coincidence as her Yorkshire Terrier Margo has pupped. Suggests her niece could have one or even two of said offspring. Anticipate what Beloved Husband will say at suggestion. He once described Margo as a hairy rat which his hunting dogs would 'delight in dispatching'.

DH shows me puppies which do indeed resemble rats but hairless ones. Do not say so to DH as think in her eyes these are substitutes for babies and do not want to hurt her feelings.

We eat delicious cake, drink sherry and play rummy whilst debating who we think is the most handsome gentleman hereabouts (aside from our husbands of course). Captain Rainer or our local member of Parliament, Gerald are our top choices. After much time we decide on CR by a whisker - his regimentals clinching it. Both agree Freddie is also worthy of note and such a kind man too.

March 6th

Glorious morning ride with Dear Hattie, Captain Rainer and a young admirer of DH's - he is besotted with her and follows her like a devoted puppy. He must be all of seventeen! Still it is nice that my sister can still attract the eye of a good looking young man.

Spring is just around the corner I feel sure.

March 7th

Heavy snow overnight.

March 8th

New governess for Darling Daughter Clemmie arrives. Miss Fairly comes with an exceptional letter of recommendation which is most encouraging. She tells me she is from Derbyshire and is an orphan. Before his death her father was a vicar. When I tell DH this she laughs and says she sounds as if she has just stepped out of the pages of 'A Lady's' novel. Am at first puzzled by this statement but then DH explains. Am at a loss of how to respond so change the subject and ask if she knows who it is Poor Lucy Smythe is having an *affaire* with. DH says she has no idea but thinks Poor Lucy craves attention so much we should be on our guard for our own husbands. Am most surprised by this observation as had not thought Poor Lucy would be so inclined. Will make sure to watch Spencer in her company from now on.

March 9th

Darling Daughter Clemmie tells me Miss Fairly has begun reading Children's and Household Tales to her. It is a collection of German fairy stories she informs me. Am not sure what to make of this as had not expected an English governess to be a fan of German literature. DDC also presents a sampler she is working which appears to be full of knots on the reverse side.

After luncheon seek out Miss Fairly in newly equipped school room. She assures me the Brothers Grimm fairy stories are 'most educational'. Say how I am keen DDC learns the 'Three R's' and does not waste her time on foreign folklore. When she points out the 'first R' is reading I counter she should be reading *English* books not frivolous stories of dubious origin. Miss Fairly stands corrected but suggests I 'look over' the book. In fairness I agree as recall she came with excellent references and I failed to finish my own schooling. Take book and place it on the pile with Poor Lucy's offerings.

March 10th

Little Charles suffering streaming cold after dim-witted nursemaid took him out for a walk - in this weather! Fear the girl is a simpleton without any common sense whatsoever.

Spencer joins us in the drawing room as I am remonstrating with Miss Grimes, who is of course sniffling. BH never can cope with tears and so then undoes all my lecturing by saying he knows she didn't mean Little Charles to catch a cold. After the nursemaid leaves tell him I am astonished at his attitude. Does he think it right his son could have caught his death due to Miss Grimes' negligence? Spencer says I am overreacting and son is only suffering a snuffle and it will harden him up! Further harsh words are exchanged and I leave him in no doubt that he will not be welcome in my bedchamber for the foreseeable future.

March 11th

Little Charles still has a chill. Miss Grimes is avoiding me as well she might.

March 12th

Darling Daughter Clemmie says she would like a kitten. Remind her she had asked for a puppy only last week to which she replies ideally she would like both. Think possibility of either slim but do not want to upset her so change the subject.

Note: Extraordinary how children these days think presents to commemorate birthdays necessary. I do not recall ever having birthday gift until I reached my majority.

March 13th

Weather has turned mild and clement. Spring definitely on its way now as see evidence of daffodils all about the parkland.

March 14th

Persistent rain ALL day long.

March 15th

Spencer Jnr has caught Little Charles' cold. The nursemaid was up all night tending to the needs of Son and Heir. Eldest son is just like his papa and is fractious and demanding when ill. Serves her right. Notice how Little Charles takes after me and suffers in silence, bless his dear heart.

March 16th

Dinner for sixteen goes not at all badly except for capons are as tough as old boots (another one of Agnes's little sayings). Sadly Gerald unable to make an appearance but Captain Rainer more than made up for his absence. What an entertaining and erudite man he is and so good looking. On first meeting had him down as one to keep my eye on; his conversation was somewhat over familiar even to my liberal mind. However, I quickly changed my opinion when I got to know him a little better. Now I see he is a man of some substance. I admire him very much.

Query: Might it not be amusing to make a scrapbook of interesting little sayings? Friends and acquaintances could be asked to contribute. Captain Rainer would be sure to supply a witty contribution. Agnes alone could provide many I feel sure.

March 17th

When he calls unexpectedly, invite Captain Rainer to supply a saying for the scrapbook I am about to start. He tells me he will give it some thought and will let me know when he has come up with something suitably amusing. Later, when Treasured Spinster Friend calls ask her to do the same. However, the best she can do is 'life is full of faradiddles' which is lame yet apt as some of the gossip she peddles is mostly a tissue of lies.

March 18th

Heavy snowfall keeps us housebound. Very inconvenient as we had planned to take luncheon with the Pascoes and dine with Freddie and Gwendolyn. No doubt Cook will be put out at the extra work caused by the inclement weather. Will look forward to indifferent meals until the weather allows us to venture forth.

Note: Tell Cook only to send six courses whilst we are alone - am pleased with self for idea.

Decide enforced withdrawal from all society is good opportunity to begin broadening one's mind with edifying book. First glance through heap that Poor Lucy loaned me but nothing captures my interest. Search library until come across the Waverly novels which I have heard ladies rave about. Am immediately daunted by tome - as alternative take up slim volume of poetry by Wordsworth. This will surely enhance knowledge. Read one or two of the shorter poems.

Later, enthused by Wordsworth descriptions of the Lake District suggest to Spencer we might take trip to the Lakes in the summer. Confused ten minutes ensues in which BH says we cannot possibly afford foreign travel this year despite his business success. Point out I mean the English Lakes and not as he mistakenly thinks, the Italian. No definite conclusion arrived at as to whether sojourn will be attempted.

Darling Daughter Clemmie recites all of three times table when she comes down with Miss Grimes and Miss Fairly before bed. Spencer Jnr, never one to be sidelined says, 'that is nothing' as he knows ALL his tables up to twelve. After he gets to his four times table Spencer steps in and tells him he is indeed a genius. I notice BH fails to mention that his daughter too is a clever girl.

Little Charles has a new tooth Miss Grimes tells us. That possibly explains why his cheeks are so red.

At dinner Spencer demands to know why we are on short rations.

March 19th

Still snowing. Children return from garden soaking wet where they have been bombarding each other with snowballs encouraged by Spencer who behaves worse than the children. Little Charles and I watch from the library as the children charge about acting like savages. Both children far too excited to be brought down again before bed.

Miss Grimes will be penning her resignation as I write after I warned her not to let the children get wet lest they catch their death. Spencer of course over-ruled me and insisted they all go out in the snow despite a blizzard almost blowing the trees flat. I saw for certain he encouraged Spencer Jnr to throw a snowball at Miss Grimes when her back was turned. If she does go I shall remember the incident and lay the blame firmly at Spencer's door.

March 20th

Snow has turned to ice making it impossible to leave the house. Spend some time collecting amusing sayings for my scrapbook. Agnes supplies me with several which I put in immediately. Ask my beloved for one but he says, somewhat crossly, he cannot 'conjure up humorous anecdotes from thin air'.

Eventually am forced to take up Mansfield Park. Realise why so far I cannot like the book, the reason being I cannot feel sympathy for Fanny Price. She appears singularly lacking in vigour and vitality. What a timid, shrinking violet she is and not *my* idea of a heroine at all. The author would have done well to choose Dear Hattie as a champion; at least she has spark, a handsome husband and interesting relations. The last time I saw Gerald he suggested I read Sense and Sensibility, far superior to Mansfield Park he tells me. Intend to take his advice as it cannot be as boring (or long) as the author's last book.

Suggest to Spencer that we play cards to pass the time. Unedifying afternoon results as he is a bad loser. To sweeten his ill temper I offer a different game which he immediately takes as invitation and makes unseemly remark. Decide to give in to BH's demands like a good wife. Time passes quickly thereafter.

March 21st

Send Agnes to bookshop for copy of Sense and Sensibility only to find when she has gone it was in the pile Poor Lucy loaned me.

March 22nd

Miss Fairly says Darling Daughter Clemmie is turning into a 'gifted' musician. I say she takes after me but when DDC scratches out excruciating sound on viola suggest governess concentrates on the pianoforte as more suitable instrument.

Reminded I have not played for a while so spend happy hour with Beethoven. Am certain if only I had the time would be proficient - or at the very least capable. Also tinkle on the harp but it is so long since I played I cannot remember any tune whatsoever. When did memory become so bad I ask myself?

Partake of an alcoholic beverage of my own devising which consists of warm claret with honey, just the thing to ward of chills.

March 23rd

The snow has at last cleared but in its stead there is slush which makes walking hazardous and certain to ruin any footwear one might don. Still at least a carriage ride to call upon Dear Hattie is now possible.

I had not known Hugo Bright was staying at High Brow House and so it came as a lovely surprise to find him there. Other guests snowed in include friends of Dear Hattie's from Cheshire - have met them before but they are not to my liking. Treasured Spinster Friend also present, she has walked to High Brow - in this weather!

Hugo and I find a quiet corner and as always talk about all things frivolous; what a relief not to have to discuss

France, political issues and books. When I tell him how I would like to take a walking tour of the Lake District he looks down his long nose and says warningly, 'walking without a purpose is a complete waste of anyone's time, especially a lady's'. He goes on to suggest I take a sedan up any incline I may aspire to climb which sets me to giggling at the very thought of it. Hugo is always a breath of fresh air. I like him very much.

After luncheon (delicious) Spencer announces we are to take a walking tour of the Lake District in July and asks Dear Hattie and William if they would like to accompany us! It is all settled amicably and my sister and I spend the rest of the afternoon planning the itinerary.

Am pleased with self; the reason we are to visit the lakes is because of my new found love of reading. Wordsworth, I tell all who will listen, is a true poet. Ah, to view the crags, pikes and silvery lakes as described by the great man, I say. Are the names not lyrical I ask; Helvellyn, Borrowdale, Bassenthwaite and Scafell.

Now travel as well as reading will broaden my horizons.

Note: Will need new wardrobe for walking trip. Also am determined to invite Hugo to Upshot Hall soon, but not at the same time as the Duchess of Lancaster.

March 24th

Ask dressmaker to make garments suitable for walking trip in shades of green and heather. Express wish for hats to be decorated with feathers from country birds such as pheasant or grouse. Am determined to look the part. One can still be fashionable and elegant even when on a walking holiday.

March 25th

Spencer mysteriously absent overnight.

March 26th

Beloved Husband returned this afternoon looking sheepish and telling me how much he admires and loves me. Expect he has been drawing the bustle too freely as usual. Will we ever be solvent?

March 27th

Hair refuses to curl no matter how hard Agnes tries. She suggests I purchase new hair tongs but cannot see how this will help. Old tongs are not so very old. She tells me I should 'eat my crusts' which truly baffles me until she explains. Her mother used to tell Agnes that eating crusts would make her hair curl. How quaint the lower orders can be. Send to kitchen for bread.

Look a complete fright at the Pascoe's supper party. Notice how everyone else's hair is beautifully dressed. Will send Agnes to purchase new tongs tomorrow, it being preferable to eating crusts.

March 28th

Housekeeper tells me Miss Grimes is over feeding the children. Check with nursemaid that children are receiving three meals a day. She assures me they are but thinks Spencer Jnr in particular needs regular 'top ups' between meals.

Summon Housekeeper who then blames Cook who reportedly says she spends all day preparing food solely for the children. Cannot get to the bottom of this so ask to see Miss Fairly as she is a sensible young lady and must know what Darling Daughter Clemmie eats at the very least. She tells me DDC has her meals in the day nursery but has a mid morning break of milk and biscuits. I think this not unreasonable and so decide to ignore Housekeeper. I am far too busy to give the matter anymore thought.

Mem: Another day dress will be needed for the lake trip in case the weather is inclement. Dove grey with a hint of mauve would look well.

March 29th

Dined at Lady V's. At dinner am sat with Lord Coniston to my right and The Old Colonel to my left. I swear Lady V does the seating plan especially to put me out of humour. The last three times we have dined at Highbourne House I have been forced to bandy words with The Old Colonel. He can always be relied upon to have me yawning through the first course and so am glad when we turn table and Lord Coniston can take up the conversation. We talk about Spencer's ability at billiards (say did not know he was proficient at the game even though he spends hours playing) and a new painting Lord Coniston acquired when in Italy.

Say how I would dearly love to visit the country to which he replies it would be a mistake to go in the summer months as it is far too hot for ladies. He goes on to suggest the spring would be the perfect time for a visit and that I must see Florence as the architecture is 'sublime'. Remember Mr Howard saying the self same thing at his talk on Italy. Manage to dredge up intelligent snippets from the talk which make me sound far better informed than I actually am.

March 30th

Fired up with last night's conversation with Lord Coniston, order book about Italy in case we are ever in a position to visit. Cannot see that this will ever be possible as we hardly ever have sixpence with which to scratch. I should like to eat pasta with Italians with fiery temperaments in pleasant sunshine whilst gazing upon fine buildings. Should I learn the language just in case a miracle happens and solvency is achieved before I am too old to travel abroad?

March 31st

At Dear Hattie's tell her of interesting conversation with Lord Coniston about Italy. Say how I long to visit the country and how I would love to learn the language. She tells me - and how she knows I forget to ask - that Lord Coniston was 'connected' to an Italian countess in his younger days and undoubtedly speaks the language fluently. DH spears me with such a look that I immediately understand her meaning. My Lord has the look of a man of experience. He is known to be fairly flush in the pockets and so has probably kept a Cytherean or two in his younger days. Then DH remembers there is an Italian phrase book in the library and despatches a footman to find it. When it arrives we try out a few words but without direction it is nigh on impossible to decide how to pronounce 'buon giorno' which is a simple Italian greeting. DH says we should try to find someone to teach us, which I agree would be the best course of action. Any tutor we find will of course, have to be funded by DH as am once again purse pinched.

April

April 1ˢᵗ

Darling Daughter Clemmie delighted with gift which is not a puppy or a kitten but a pony of her very own. When I find out, too late, Spencer has purchased this extravagant gift he defends his decision vigorously. Says she has been sharing Spencer Jnr's mount and this has led to arguments so 'one stone two birds'.

I see how this gift is not only a present for DDC but also a way of rewarding precious Son and Heir. Later overhear Spencer Jnr complaining his pony is inferior to DDC's and that he should have new, larger, faster mount. Decide against telling Spencer as the child can wrap his father around his little finger and before I know it Spencer Jnr will be riding an Arab thoroughbred.

April 2ⁿᵈ

DDC informs me she has named her pony Napoleon.

Query: Is this not unpatriotic and should I suggest she rename pony Wellington?

April 3rd

Little Charles able to walk a few steps unaided Miss Grimes says when she presents the children to us before bed. However, Little Charles refuses to comply and sits on the rug petulantly refusing to demonstrate newly acquired skill. Say how Darling Daughter Clemmie walked sooner than either boy to which Spencer replies 'bunkum'. Decide Spencer has selective memory especially where Son and Heir concerned. Do not pass on this information as it would surely result in an unedifying argument. During my marriage I have learnt which battles to fight and which to pass over.

April 4th

Begin reading Sense and Sensibility and find I like it much better than Mansfield Park. The two heroines appear not to be half as wet as Fanny Price thank goodness.

April 5th

Luncheon with the Pascoes to make up for the one we missed due to snow. Good food and company all the more welcome after being imprisoned for days. Everyone affable and in good spirits now we are unconfined.

Nigella Pascoe tells me, in confidential tones, that Gerald and Mariah are to be in London for the foreseeable future. As a member of Parliament Gerald is often away from Killinghall when the house sits so why she thinks she has to deliver this news in conspiratorial manner is beyond reason. However, what *I* know and what Nosy Nigella does not is the reason *why* Mariah is to be with her husband this session.

April 6th

Fitzroy showed great interest in my piano playing at last night's musical evening at Lady V's - insisted on turning the pages as I played. He himself has splendid singing voice. Found myself quite overcome when he sang, 'Soldier's Adieu'. Beloved Husband has a beautiful tenor voice but never ventures to sing in public, more's the pity.

April 7th

Moorlands. Dear Hattie and I spend the day perusing the elegant shops of Harrogate. Resign myself to the fact that money must be spent if I am to look half way decent on our trip to the Lakes. With Indian muslin at ten shillings a yard this will not be an easy task.

We are to stay overnight at Moorlands. How I wish we had a town house in Harrogate, or anywhere else for that matter. Chances of visiting Italy are remote when cannot even afford staying in Harrogate unless at DH's expense.

We are both fitted for new boots, essential for our walking trip we are told. The shoemaker says we shall have to 'wear them in' before departing. We both agree the boots are not as elegant as we would like but the cobbler assures us we will need footwear of a substantial nature for our hikes. He insists even a small heel is out of the question.

April 8th

Dear Hattie and I ride out on the Stray where all the fashionable people are parading either on foot, on horseback or in their carriages. See several noteworthy coats of arms as carriages glide by. Numerous acquaintances of DH's (mainly gentleman) approach us and an agreeable morning is had by all. I should like to live in town, one gets to meet an interesting assortment of people.

Later, spot Lady V exiting a tearoom on Montpelier Street but manage to avoid her by darting into the haberdashers. She is with a gentleman of middling years and is quite unusually flushed and animated. The gentleman is oddly familiar to me. DH says she could not see him clearly as I had propelled her into the shop before she had chance to notice him.

Purchase beautiful set of mother of pearl buttons before leaving the establishment.

Luncheon taken with several singularly interesting gentlemen. The ladies present are all dressed beautifully and I feel decidedly drab by comparison. Might I get a Harrogate modiste to make me something for the new season?

One of our party shows more than a passing interest in Dear Hattie. Later ask sister if she is inclined in that direction but she guffaws loudly and assures me the gentleman is nothing but a small flirtation as she is madly in love with her husband.

Query: Is it not possible to be madly in love with one's

husband and still enjoy a diversion?

I shall give the answer serious thought when I have the time.

April 9th

Spend enjoyable but exhausting afternoon practising country dances. Dear Hattie, of course, has a dance teacher - only wish we could afford a man to teach myself and Darling Daughter Clemmie. Dancing teacher is French (naturally) and quite accomplished despite being a corpulent little man. He sports a trim moustache which is possibly stuck on - this according to DH. When it is my turn to dance with him almost fall over own feet so intent am I trying to see if moustache is real or not. Dare not glance in DH's direction otherwise fit of giggles will render me senseless.

When Monsieur takes his leave we conclude the facial hair is real but waxed. The French are an odd people despite being at the forefront of all things stylish.

Mem: Try to keep in mind steps to the new dance so can coach Darling Daughter Clemmie myself.

Enchanting evening at Moorlands spent with many Artistic Types and a smattering of handsome officers who are all attentive and keen to entertain us.

April 10th

Upshot Hall. Ask myself whether Housekeeper has been practically laying in wait all the time I have been in Harrogate as she greets me before I have time to reach the house. Am informed in solemn voice that a kitchen maid is with child and has been let go. This is her big news? The woman is beyond the pale.

April 11th

Dear Hattie not at all her self today. She is quite distracted and melancholic. Most unlike her usual sunny disposition. Firstly, she declines to even glance at the fashion plates in my latest edition of The Lady's Monthly Museum - odd as she usually devours it (I know for certain she has not yet seen it). Secondly, when I regale her with Treasured Spinster Friend's latest gossip she does not ask a single question, even when it is evident parts of the scandal are extremely unlikely.

Am really quite worried about my sister.

April 12th

Call at High Brow House on my way to see Old Governess. Try to persuade sister to accompany me on my mercy mission - Miss Step has been unwell - but Dear Hattie cannot be prevailed upon to leave the house so low is her mood. This is so unlike her, usually she can be cajoled out of her ill humour but of late she seems preoccupied and a little distant.

April 13th

Spencer says he has lost his favourite snuff box. Point out as he never takes snuff it is of no import. He says that is not the point. Ask him what is the point to which he replies if I do not understand then he cannot be bothered to explain.

Husbands are the most infuriating creatures.

April 14th

Dear Hattie calls, pitches herself dramatically like a felled tree on the chaise and says she is convinced William will 'do away' with her if she does not provide expected son and heir soon. See at once what has been on DH'S mind of late.

Reassure her this is complete nonsense as A) The Duke is besotted with her and B) she is a healthy young woman and in no time will have more children than any reasonable lady would know what to do with. Say gaily she will have so many heirs and spares she will rival the vicar's wife. Say also I understand her concern but assure her it is still early days and she should not worry in the least. She points out I was with child within weeks of marrying Spencer, a fact which I cannot deny, but again attempt to assure her all will be well.

Several hours pass before finally convince DH she is being unduly sensitive. She is quite cheerful when she leaves after luncheon.

Later get to thinking about DH's Unfortunate Situation. Reluctantly admit to self she is right to be concerned. It is odd to think my sister could be barren. *I* have never had a problem conceiving; in fact Spencer Jnr may have been in evidence *before* I married. Can understand DH's concern but cannot say so to her face, she is already at her wit's end. The Duke *will* of course want a son and heir to carry on his ancient family name; it is expected. But although their marriage is a love match, without an heir where does that leave DH?

Answer comes there none.

April 15th

Captain Rainer calls ostensibly to see Beloved Husband but is unlucky and so Fitz makes do with me. What a welcome addition to our little society he is; so handsome, charming and witty. I do like a man who can make one laugh. Many are the single young ladies setting their cap at him I would wager. How he has escaped marriage thus far I cannot say as he must be in his late twenties and is immensely eligible. Not all military men are keen to take a wife I know. They like to travel unburdened possibly or perhaps they are reluctant to take a wife in case they are lost in action. I will ask him when I get to know him a little better; would not want to appear like Lady V who demands to know the most intimate details about even mere acquaintances.

Will also ask about the conflicts in which the captain has been involved - The Duke says they fought alongside each other at Waterloo - all this to broaden my mind of course. Recently I feel like a sponge just waiting to soak up knowledge.

Ask Fitz if he speaks Italian. He does not but says he can 'get by' in French. BH can more than get by in French so that is nothing to write home about. Any fool can speak French. Admit to feeling a little disappointed in CR on this occasion.

April 16th

Fitz calls again and redeems himself somewhat in my estimations. After an interesting discussion about several skirmishes and campaigns in which he was involved, he tells me about Waterloo which of course I was most keen to hear about. The Old Colonel never made his stories *half* so interesting. However, CR makes the battle sound quite horrible - am sure I should not like to meet a Frenchman. Italian gentlemen would not be so brutal, of that I am certain - have been led to believe (by no other than Hugo) that Italian men are all romantics like Casanova.

Fitz then takes up my copy of Milton, which I happen to have left laying about but he dismisses it out of hand. I do like a man who has an opinion. I also like a man who reads, all Spencer ever picks up is The Times and the latest scandal sheet.

Fitz goes on to mention a book entitled 'The Monk'. Say, foolishly, I have never heard of Matthew Gregory Lewis. Yet again literary ignorance is an embarrassment - for once do not even try to pretend I know anything about the author as am sure will be caught out in a lie and appear even more idiotic. Fitz raises an eyebrow and offers to lend me his copy as he thinks I will enjoy it above all else. Why the raised eyebrow? We take a little walk about the water gardens. The fresh air and the company are most invigorating but then it comes on to rain and we are forced back indoors. As CR leaves he says he will see me later - and bring The Monk with him - I had invited him to dine -

had completely forgotten Spencer away overnight on 'important estate business'.

April 17th

Ride out with Dear Hattie whom I tell about last night's dinner guest. She adopts horrified look, warns me to be careful regarding Captain Rainer then giggles and asks for 'all the juicy details'.

Ask her if she has any news. She says she has not.

Later begin reading The Monk ...

April 18th

Try once again to make inroads into The Monk but fail to see how CR thinks the book is entertaining.

April 19th

The hunt gathers at Dear Hattie's but she does not accompany The Duke. Speculate whether her Unfortunate Situation is at last resolved. She is a great one for hunting so cannot understand why she stays behind with me. Am of course most keen to ask her about her condition but know she will tell me when she is ready.

Captain Rainer, we both notice, has an excellent seat.

April 20th

Feel unable to rise from my bed until after midday. Blame Dear Hattie for this state of affairs. She knows I cannot resist temptation and would insist on opening far more bottles of wine than was good for us yesterday.

Spencer again away overnight on 'important estate business', so after dining at Upshot Hall DH stays the night. As always we revert to our childhood habit of sharing a bed and talk late into the night about the gentlemen in our lives, this season's latest fashions and whether we will ever get to visit Italy. There is no reason of course why DH cannot go to Italy, she and William are more than comfortably off. Am touched when she says she wants the four of us to visit Italy together so we can have a 'great adventure'. Sigh when reflect on state of finances which will not allow a trip anytime soon.

DH as always warms her freezing cold feet on me, a thing she has done since we were children. Feel quite sorry for The Duke if he now has to shoulder this load. No wonder she is not with child – it is enough to cool anyone's ardour.

April 21st

Spencer still from home. Is it too much to ask for him to send a note to say he is not DEAD?

April 22nd

Housekeeper asks if I am aware the butcher, fishmonger and grocer are refusing to extend credit until outstanding bills are paid IMMEDIATELY. Notice how Housekeeper has keen sense of the dramatic.

Am called upon to produce forty shillings and nine pence if butcher is to be placated. Go to safe for coin only to find there is none. Not a single guinea. Tell Housekeeper the monies will be forthcoming tomorrow but cannot imagine how.

Spencer returned from 'important estate business' is eventually run to ground examining his favourite hunter's hind quarters. Ask why the safe is empty of cash. He adopts look of astonishment and says how should he know? A heated exchange ensues in which BH denies all knowledge of the twenty guineas we agreed should be kept for emergencies. He goes as far as to say current lack of coin to pay for household necessities is not an emergency. Make suggestion he ride over to Bankwell Hall and solicit coin from his brother Freddie if he wishes to eat at all this week. Spencer says there is absolutely no need as he will be able to produce money for creditors by tomorrow. We both know this will not be the case. Depending for financial security on the throw of a dice or the turn of a card is not the answer, I inform him curtly. BH as always is unperturbed and adds, 'Why all the fuss when we can always dine out at Dear Hattie's or Freddie's or at a push Lady V's'.

With great difficulty refrain from setting about him with a riding crop.

April 23rd

Am refusing to speak to Spencer until he becomes a more responsible Husband and Father.

April 24th

Emeralds are once again residing at pawn broker in Harrogate. Think regretfully how they visit the town more often than I.

April 25th

The Monk is not the gripping 'Gothic Horror' Captain Rainer led me to believe. I enjoy a Gothic novel - I have been known to pick up a book by Mrs Radcliffe - as well as the next lady but this offering is heavy going to my discerning eye. Then I notice the passages he has thoughtfully marked out for me and all becomes clear - then cannot put the book down. Understand now why Fitz raised an eyebrow - I raised two. After I read aloud some of the more salacious passages Dear Hattie is of course desperate to read it too.

April 26th

Hear from several sources (none of which are Treasured Spinster Friend) that Miss Shaw has returned to Thirsk.

At last.

April 27th

Miss Fairly says Darling Daughter Clemmie is able to recite poetry at will when she has been set a task. I say she gets this skill from me as I could do the same at her age.

Why I cannot now is a moot point.

Spend unedifying half hour trying to commit to memory

a verse by Lord Byron but no sooner am I convinced I have it down pat it drains clean away again.

April 28th

Lady V calls and drops into conversation that Hugo Bright is second cousin to the Duchess of Lancaster. Try not to look horrified and say she must be mistaken as Hugo is always so disparaging of the lady and especially her dress sense. 'Exactly,' says Lady V in tone resembling utter contempt, 'we cannot choose our relations'. Am completely baffled by this exchange and so offer her tea, praying cook will serve something half way decent alongside it.

Note: Speak to Cook. Biscuits yet again verging on inedible; very nearly broke a tooth!

April 29th

Dear Hattie says she has searched but cannot find suitable person to teach us Italian. There are any number of gentlemen who could teach us Russian apparently but as neither of us has any desire to visit the country then this is of no account. Try out various phrases from DH's Italian phrase book but give up after half an hour.

April 30th

DH and I write to The Lady to ask if they know of suitable teacher of Italian who might reside close to Harrogate. Do not hold out much hope.

May

May 1ˢᵗ

Miss Grimes tells me Spencer Jnr is becoming 'self willed'. Think to mention to Spencer before eldest son becomes unmanageable. The nursemaid catches me as I am about to meet Treasured Spinster Friend for a ride out. Ask governess what behaviour in particular she is against. She cannot specify particulars but says in general terms Son and Heir tends towards stubbornness and does not comply with rules willingly. Say I will speak to him on my return.

Make the mistake of telling TSF about Spencer Jnr's lapse in behaviour. She spends entire ride telling me how to rectify the matter. Goes on to say unless I put my foot down with a firm hand the boy will, 'ride roughshod over you all'.

Query: How would SHE know? TSF is a SPINSTER and therefore without a HUSBAND *or* CHILDREN. Only kindness at her plight stops me from pointing this out. At her age she will never catch a husband now and for this I am truly sorry but every now and then she goes too far.

On return to Upshot Hall tell Spencer of his eldest son's misconduct and suggest the boy needs the firm hand only a father can provide if this behaviour is to be nipped in the bud. Spencer agrees and says he will speak to Son and Heir later. Why not now I ask? Strike while the iron is hot. Spencer says he is 'busy' and will go to nursery before the boy is given his supper. Suggest son is put to bed *without* supper if he does not appear chastened after reprimand. Am mollified when Spencer agrees whole-heartedly.

Later outside the nursery hear squeals of laughter from within. Am curious to see what all the noise is about. On opening the nursery door see BH on hands and knees being 'ridden' by Spencer Jnr and encouraged by Darling Daughter Clemmie who is brandishing a riding crop dangerously in the air. Little Charles is red in the face and waving a flag shouting what I think are the words, 'faster faster faster' - the child's speech is still at a rudimentary stage so some of his utterances are naturally indistinct.

In our bedchamber words are exchanged regarding Spencer's parenting methods. BH maintains it is the fault of the governess and suggests strongly she should be replaced forthwith. Spencer Jnr is 'so full of fun' BH says, adding he was just the same at Son and Heir's age. He asks, 'Did I turn out so bad?'

Forbear to comment.

Am convinced Miss Grimes will resign, so leave to change for dinner before I say something I may regret.

May 2nd

Miss Grimes gives notice.

May 3rd

Finish The Monk. When I try to give the copy back to Fitz he insists I keep it and think of him ... again the raised eyebrow which makes him appear so devilishly attractive. After we take a turn about the drawing room we 'lose' ourselves in the library - how apt.

May 4th

Receive letter from Mama saying Georgiana is coming to stay with us and that my youngest sister will arrive on Friday. Am sent reeling as l realise today is indeed Friday.

Tell Spencer of sister's impending visit. He says nothing then thinks again and replies it will be 'company for you'. Am astonished when five minutes later Georgiana bursts into the room unannounced and states categorically that she is 'fagged to death', Mama is a 'harridan' and she is never going home *ever* again.

Spencer rises from the sofa, welcomes Georgiana and then looking at me says cryptically, 'I will leave you to it'.

May 5th

Georgiana spends several hours telling me her woes which are many and varied.

May 6th

Dear Hattie pays a call and Georgie repeats her grievances but with added dramatic flourishes, flashes of anger and interspersed with tears.

Georgie is 'old' for her age DH says when we are at last alone. Georgie having stormed out of the morning room when not receiving the sympathy she thought her due. I agree but add she is remarkably immature at the same time, which is, we both agree quite disconcerting. Do I know, DH says, she will run rings around me if I let her?

Mem: Consult Old Governess regarding Georgie's behaviour. Am sure she will have pearls of wisdom about how to temper Georgie's more extreme outbursts.

May 7th

Agnes informs me Georgie, who is surprisingly tall for a girl of her age, has ransacked my wardrobe and left clothes strewn on the bed and worse, also on the floor. Chide myself as did say Georgie could borrow something to wear to Dear Hattie's this evening.

Later find her 'dolled up to the nines' - a phrase Mama has acquired from a Scottish lady of her acquaintance - it is a saying she uses when a lady has tried too hard to impress with her attire. Tell Georgie to change at once and receive what I can only describe as a bad tempered tirade. Am forced to say she will not accompany us to DH's if she carries on in this disgraceful, ill-mannered way. At once she changes her tune and becomes quiet and compliant. Later tell Spencer the girl simply needs discipline. BH is unconvinced.

At bedtime Agnes tells me Georgiana asked her to 'pinch' a pair of my best silk stockings for her to wear. The girl is incorrigible and will come to a bad end I am convinced.

May 8th

Interview totally unsuitable woman to take over from Miss Grimes. Am at wits end thinking of ways to procure new nursemaid.

May 9th

Georgiana has to be restrained from partaking of too much claret at dinner. Dear Hattie and I agree we shall have to keep a close eye on the girl. We thought we were a trifle wayward in our day but Georgiana is totally uninhibited in her behaviour. She also has a very free way of speaking, especially to gentlemen, which is indecorous in one so young. Her popular phrase of the moment, a phrase I find quite vulgar, is 'fagged to death'. She uses this with gusto to describe how she feels several times a day. Surely one so young cannot be 'fagged to death' all day and all night? Another of her favourite idioms is 'fair gutfounded' which she says an hour after she has eaten an enormous meal; how she can be hungry all the time is also beyond me. Where she picks up such vulgar sayings I cannot imagine - not at school as she has been expelled. Will once again ask her to moderate her language but fear any request will fall on deaf ears.

May 10th

Georgiana begs Spencer to teach her how to play faro. I *insist* he does not. This culminates in a door being loosened from its hinges as Georgie storms out of the room in a huff.

Write to Mama and hint Spencer not keen on Georgiana staying more than two weeks. This is untruth but know Mama will take not a bit of notice if I object to sister staying the entire summer. My nerves are already in shreds. Having Georgie in the house is like having a particularly badly trained mastiff running free. One never knows when it will bite.

May 11th

Dear Hattie, Georgie and I pay a morning call on latest incumbent at New Park - Miss Shaw has indeed left Killinghall.

Mrs Flight (lemon muslin with sheer sleeves) is a widow - a young attractive widow I might add. She appears very comfortably off and informs us she has recently returned north from London having wintered abroad. She is here as she used to live in the area as a child she tells us; her father, a colonel with the militia, was stationed hereabouts. Talk about Mrs Flight's young son - 'Such a Treasure', London life and *our* Old Colonel who is a family friend of hers apparently.

On the ride home Georgie announces she hopes when she marries, her husband will 'drop dead' soon after the nuptials so she can have some 'fun'. Ask her what on earth she can mean. She explains, misguidedly in my opinion, that widows have much more freedom than wives, sisters or daughters who are ruled by their men folk. 'Widows', she tells us wisely, are 'not expected to answer to any man and so can please themselves'.

Concede to self the wisdom of this remark, but then feel instant regret as would not be without my Beloved Husband for anything. I can see Dear Hattie is mortified but says nothing.

May 12th

Georgie and I walk into the village and bump into Lady V. Greetings are exchanged, then Lady V compliments youngest sister on her complexion and her outfit in most effusive manner. Georgie beams and returns the compliment in glowing terms so that I am quite taken aback by her sincerity and eloquence. As we move off to continue our shopping Georgie says 'what a stupid old trout'. Point out Lady V is not as old as Mama to which Georgie replies 'all people over forty should be shot'. Refrain to make comment at this remarkable statement. Young ladies have so many opinions these days.

May 13th

Spencer is teaching Georgie archery. Not altogether sure this is a good idea. She will probably take it upon herself to eliminate old people willy nilly. Watch out Lady V.

May 14th

Luncheon taken at Bankwell Hall. Gwen once again over-dressed in unflattering shade of puce which is trimmed to within an inch of its life with white lace - even her hair is festooned with what appears to be the trimming from a lamp shade.

On the way home Georgie states emphatically she would not live with Gwendolyn for her weight in gold but that Freddie is a different matter all together. Cannot think of suitable reply to this extraordinary announcement so let it pass.

Later, on reflection decide Georgiana is far too fond of airing her views without due regard to others. Must certainly make the time to dissuade her from these unbecoming outbursts. The girl needs to mind her manners, especially in company otherwise she will compromise herself and more to the point our family. Can see all too clearly why Mama has sent her away.

May 15th

'The Lucky Widow', as Georgie disrespectfully calls Mrs Flight, returns our call (apple green day dress with long sleeves). Dear Hattie arrives as tea is served and says what a lovely surprise to see Mrs Flight again. Georgie and I both know this is a fabrication as DH is an open book to us. Why DH has taken against the widow I cannot say. We talk about our children - the widow has only one son as her husband was *taken* when she was one and twenty. Had he lived she informs us, she would have produced at least five more children by now. 'Theo - Such a Treasure' was a 'bridal tour' baby she announces proudly.

Am obliged to glare at youngest sister who tries, and fails, to suppress unbecoming giggle. Cannot help but think this kind of talk inappropriate in front of a girl of Georgiana's age and disposition. Also feel for Dear Hattie in her Unfortunate Situation at the turn the discussion has taken. Mrs Flight clearly has a London frame of mind and thinks no subject off limits, a fact I find most disconcerting. Georgiana is easily led as it is so this kind of loose talk can only set her the wrong example.

Note: Speak to Georgie privately regarding suitable topics for conversation pointing out she should not hold Mrs Flight up as worthy of emulation.

When Mrs Flight takes her leave, DH says she cannot warm to the woman but is at a loss to understand why. It is simply a *feeling* she says. Georgie finishes off the biscuits and says is the feeling jealousy as The Lucky Widow can go about doing as she likes because she is a WIDOW? Remonstrate with Georgie and say this cannot be the case as DH married The Duke for love and not solely for his twenty thousand pounds a year, vast estate, his town houses and shooting lodges.

Dear Hattie lays back on the sofa and sighs meaningfully. She then leaps up, sends for more biscuits and sherry, throws a log on the fire with great energy before polishing off the lot. Remarkable!

May 16th

Spencer says Georgie making great progress with archery which is a surprise to me as youngest sister is not known for her ability to concentrate for any length of time. He has booked an archery instructor for her he informs me, as he cannot always spare the time to teach her himself.

More expense. And what message does this send the girl? That she will be residing at Upshot Hall for the foreseeable future? Remonstrate forcibly with BH but he says he thought I would be pleased. Am at a loss to understand Spencer at times and now is one of those occasions. Am truly exasperated.

May 17th

Lady V's morning call unceremoniously interrupted by Georgie brandishing a bow and arrow in totally undignified manner.

Pay visit to Old Governess (sans Georgie) and explain how younger sister's conduct is inappropriate and fear that, despite my best efforts she is playing me for a fool. When I tell her some of Georgie's more outrageous antics she laughs light-heartedly and says Dear Hattie and I were 'just the same'. Protest most effusively - am convinced we were perhaps a little frivolous but never so wayward or so outspoken. Miss Step reminds me of several 'larks' and instances of 'high spirits' which she assures me were not dissimilar to the ones Georgie is getting up to now.

Had quite forgotten about Johnny Bailey's breeching

pants and the frogs - even now I cannot help but smile at the look on his mama's face - but then think to remind Miss Step haughtily that at the time we were much, much younger than Georgiana. She then harks back to a particularly embarrassing episode in my life, a time when I thought (foolishly) I was in love with the handsome son of Papa's land steward. In a somewhat forward manner, she reminds me, I wrote to ask Frank Bates to elope - it caused all sorts of embarrassment at the time as I now recall. This incident she says was the 'final straw' and Mama packed me off to the ladies seminary shortly afterwards.

Of course I see the parallels OG is trying to draw but still maintain Georgiana will come to a bad end if not reined in soon. I say, with as much confidence as I can muster, that *I* went on to make a sound marriage, and Dear Hattie has bagged herself The Duke. Georgie will never have the opportunity of a good marriage if she carries on as she is - running amok and throwing eye at every man she sees and all without a chaperone in sight.

When Miss Step begins reminiscing about another best forgotten incident involving myself *sans* chaperone at the Spa Ball, I decide to leave. Beyond these recollections OG is no help whatsoever; she simply says Georgie will grow up to be just like Dear Hattie and I and how 'marvellous' that will be.

May 18th

Ride out with Georgiana but cannot keep pace with her. She

rides like a neck or nothing man and is lost to me when she clears a hedge and rides off into the woods without a backward glance. Return home but sister does not make an appearance for several hours. When she returns I ask her where she has been. She is at first evasive then says 'riding' in a manner that does not brook discussion.

Am quickly coming to the end of my tether.

May 19th

Georgie once again gave her chaperone the slip and went who knows where for at least three hours this afternoon. When I tell Spencer he says she is 'heading for a fall' and did I know she is keen on Captain Rainer? Am astonished at this news and immediately go in search of her. Find her thwacking the heads off the roses with a riding crop and wearing another of my day dresses. Cross words are exchanged before she turns on her heel and says 'you are beyond irritating' in tone of voice I reserve for badly behaved animals.

May 20th

Letter from Mama saying Georgiana cannot possibly come home before July as she, Mama, is going to be in Bath until then.

May 21st

Green brocade which Georgie borrowed yesterday has torn sleeve Agnes informs me.

May 22nd

Housekeeper tells me Georgiana is to be found most days after luncheon playing cards with the grooms. Send note to Dear Hattie asking her to come to Upshot so we can both remonstrate with youngest sister. DH arrives forthwith but Georgie is nowhere to be found.

May 23rd

Remind Spencer to retrieve emeralds from pawnbroker.

May 24th

Decide to give Miss Grimes one more chance. Finding a replacement is proving nigh on impossible. At first she says she cannot withdraw her resignation but then changes her mind when I promise her an extra half day. I am a fool to myself.

May 25th

Spencer rescues emeralds at eleventh hour. Nerves in shreds - mine, not his of course.

May 26th

Dine at Lady V's but do not take Georgiana with us as she cannot be trusted. Have said she is not allowed out of the house until I receive an apology for her behaviour yesterday. Freddie was marvellous and said it was just 'high spirits'. Do not think Gwen agreed.

Will be prematurely grey if Georgie stays at Upshot Hall much longer.

May 27th

Dear Hattie calls to tell me she is to throw a 'surprise' party for my birthday. Obliged to point out it can hardly be a surprise now she has told me. Agree instantly when she says idea of surprise party is good in theory but any lady of breeding wants advance warning if she is to be main attraction. Spend a happy morning discussing new gown I will need, eating crumpets and drinking a fine sherry.

May 28th

Spend time with Georgiana picking out fabrics for 'surprise' birthday gown. Give in to sister's demand and say she may order something new also, on condition she apologises to Gwendolyn. Stand over her while she writes letter saying she is deeply sorry to have caused offence. Fear, however, this will not be enough for my sister-in-law. She will possibly expect Georgie to be tarred and feathered although I can quite see how Georgie's remark was taken as criticism.

May 29th

Dinner and dancing at the Harpers. Gerald's greeting is, as usual, warm and inviting but am not entirely satisfied with his lady's welcome. Mariah receives me well enough - she is perfectly well bred, surprisingly so, yet her manner leaves much to be desired. She goes out of her way to discuss her political views with me which I've noted before are quite revolutionary. One feels one is cornered and cannot get away. At least with Lady V it is possible to move on. Consider pretending to faint as a means to escape but am saved at last moment by Gerald's intervention.

I think she does not like me. Quite bewildering.

Later on the way back home, Dear Hattie tells me about an enjoyable encounter with the new commanding officer recently arrived in Killinghall. We both agree Colonel Frasier is exceptionally handsome - and single - which is of no consequence to either of us of course.

Both also agree Georgie needs to be watched around any of the militia. She is especially attracted to men in uniform. It is true DH and I feel the same way but we are altogether more discerning in our behaviour. Georgie is flirtatious to such a degree she appears pert, a fact that has not gone unnoticed by Lady V. Tonight, much to our embarrassment, Georgie almost threw herself at a young officer. Lady V's fan practically took flight at the sight of Georgie leading him to the dance floor. Our younger sister is not at all worried about our poor opinion of her antics and when reprimanded suggested Dear Hattie and I were 'behind the times'.

Note: DH still not with child. Fear she is becoming despondent again - am at a loss of how to help her. See another visit to the spa looming.

May 30th

Georgie informs me she saw Dear Hattie and Colonel

Frasier on the Stray 'canoodling'. Had no idea Georgie had been to Harrogate in the first place. Ask youngest sister what she was doing on the Stray - also think to enquire was she chaperoned? Strongly suspect her of lying when she tells me she was accompanied by Miss Trim but as I cannot produce proof to the contrary am forced to let the matter drop.

Note: Keep closer eye on Georgiana's comings and goings. Miss Trim is most lax and not altogether quick off the mark. Mama's idea of a 'mature and stabilising' older maid not altogether a good idea, as notice Miss Trim is prone to fall asleep giving Georgiana the opportunity to give the elderly maid the slip.

Georgie's choice of word - 'canoodling' - is interesting. It could mean something different to a fifteen year old. Resolve to ask DH about Colonel Frasier.

May 31st

Without ceremony Georgie bursts in upon Gerald and I in the library when we are perusing a guide book on Italy. Thankfully we had not ventured far when we are disturbed. Without comment, but with a sly, lascivious look, she exits the room as quickly as she entered.

Spend some little time after Gerald leaves Upshot Hall thinking whether to explain situation in the library to Georgie. Decide against raising the matter as it would necessitate lying - again. She is bound to draw her own conclusions so will leave the matter in abeyance in the hope she will forget about the incident.

June

June 1st

Have ordered beautiful new gown for 'surprise' party - yellow-gold daisies on white background with long bound sleeves a' la Renaissance. Bodice and sleeve detail are gold silk, white shawl with gold fringe to match. Dainty gold slippers complete the ensemble. Shall be the height of fashion as no one, but *no one* has worn this style sleeve in our circle yet.

June 2nd

On our ride Dear Hattie adopts look of derision when I broach subject of 'canoodling' with Colonel Frasier. She assures me she has eyes only for her husband in most stern manner. She manages to say this in such a way I am forced to take offence. Sharp words are then exchanged when she mentions my 'conduct with Gerald' and 'not to mention Captain Rainer'.

Feel obliged to ride off without saying goodbye. Are both my sisters to take against me?

Later DH sends a note of apology begging forgiveness saying her nerves are on edge making her short tempered -

insists I will know the reason why she feels so put out. I do of course; she had refused tea so it may well be lack of nourishment that ails her.

June 3rd

'Surprise' party will mark my twenty seventh birthday. Where have the years gone? As I peer into looking glass, something I rarely do too closely, wonder are my best years behind me. Perhaps it is time to make concerted effort to turn back the clock or at least try to halt the decline. Decide therefore to embark on new beauty routine. Enlist the help of my maid who is most knowledgeable regarding beauty preparations. Agnes suggests massaging my face and neck with lanolin and lemon juice, the one to soften lines the other to bleach imperfections. Lemons procured from our own hot house I am pleased to note. She assures me I do not look my age but then says might she suggest it is time to consider 'enhancing' what God gave me with a little artifice. At first think to be slighted but then immediately send her on an errand to purchase the items she suggests but none of these are to be found *anywhere* in Killinghall. Concede will have to wait until am next in Harrogate to purchase said items. Most annoying as the big day of 'surprise' party is looming ever closer.

Query: Why is it as men age they become mature and sophisticated whilst we ladies merely grow old and ravaged?

June 4th

Continue with the new beauty regime but see no discernible difference in the fine lines around my eyes. Despondent, I show Agnes an article in La Belle Assemblée which proposes using their special 'Wrinkle Remedy'. It will, the piece assures, have me looking ten years younger in no time at all.

Agnes is despatched to the kitchen to make up the concoction. The article swears the ingredients will be easily obtained from my own kitchen. Cook tells Agnes we do not have at least two of the components and so Agnes is sent to the chemist shop forthwith. If am to look ten years younger for 'surprise' party then time is of the essence. On her return green unguent is plastered on face, neck and décolletage. It smells most unappealing but Agnes says I must suffer if I am to see positive results. God forbid Spencer should see me smeared like this.

June 5th

Out for a morning ride with Beloved Husband when our paths cross with Mrs Flight (deep blue riding habit with nautical looking tricorn hat). We exchange pleasantries and then are invited to intimate dinner where there will be just six if we are able to oblige her. Spencer at once accepts.

On ride back he comments what a good looking woman Mrs Flight is and how when he met her last he found her most amusing. Am startled at his confession and immediately ask when and where he had met the widow before? He narrows his brow unconvincingly, he has never been good at lying, and says he *thinks* it was at The Old Colonel's but he cannot be sure. Decide to let the matter drop - for now.

June 6th

At Dear Hattie's tell her I am in full agreement with her regarding The Lucky Widow. I too cannot like Mrs Flight no matter how hard I try. Ask how old does she suppose the lady to be? Am dismayed when she says 'younger than you' and 'definitely no older than four and twenty'.

We sit in the garden and eat cake. I ask if she intends to invite The Lucky Widow to my 'surprise' party. She says of course not and what do I take her for? Am touched by DH's loyalty and relieved beyond measure.

We talk about my new beauty regime which she immediately decides to take up. Feel slightly put out at this turn of events. DH is younger by four years so any results *I* see may be negated if she embarks on the same ritual. Immediately feel mean-spirited and so tell her the 'Wrinkle Remedy' recipe even though she has no need of it. Like Georgie she has a flawless complexion.

June 7th

On the night of the 'intimate dinner' ask Agnes to dress my hair in a different style to my usual one and to lay out my violet with silver diamante drops; am at pains to look my best or a little younger at the very least - spend almost an hour prone and smeared in green balm to this effect.

Later, Georgie stomps in and throws herself on the chaise and asks what *have* I done to my hair. Ask her, in strident tones, to leave which she does not. Say if she intends to stay then she should keep comments to herself which she does until I put on violet and diamante then she declares, 'Lord Sis that colour washes you out and ages you by at least five years'. Evict her unceremoniously from dressing room and change into my bronze.

The other guests at the 'intimate dinner' are The Old Colonel, Lady V, and Mrs Flight's 'Charming Brother Simon' (I would bet good coin he is a rake).

The meal is an elegant affair with much gold leaf in evidence on dessert pears and plums. Cannot ever recall seeing this much extravagance at a provincial gathering before and think the trimmings all rather vulgar. Spencer is delighted with everything, especially everything that passes from Mrs Flight's lips.

When the ladies leave the gentlemen to their brandy and port, Lady V tells Mrs Flight what a perfect couple Spencer and I are and what adorable children we have. The Lucky Widow says she is amazed to learn I have *three* children and is astounded the eldest is *eight*. Smile sweetly but not too much in case wrinkles make too obvious an appearance.

Am not taken in for a second by Lady V's attempts at flattery. Has the lady got wind of my 'surprise' party? If not, why then is she being so insufferably agreeable?

On the way home Spencer says he cannot remember

ever having such an enjoyable evening and is not Mrs Flight a wit. I say, truthfully, I had not noticed. Spencer then goes on to say how he felt certain we would be friends and so has invited her to my 'surprise' party.

Query: BH has shown *absolutely* no interest in my 'surprise' party thus far, so what now gives him the right to invite people without so much as a by your leave? Am furious but impotent.

June 8th

Not a cloud in the sky, warm and fine all day yet my mood is far from sunny. Steer clear of Spencer all day as fear he will receive the full force of my venom for inviting Mrs Flight and her wit!

When I suggest to Georgie she might go home after my 'surprise' party she locks herself in her room and refuses to come out. What a trying and unpredictable girl she is. Tell her it is far too hot to be indoors but she refuses to open her door. Do not see her for the rest of the day and then feel slightly guilty that am being relieved of her company. Am certain knitting brows together in consternation at Georgie's antics is adding to fine lines.

June 9th

Am distraught. Close inspection of wrinkles shows no perceptible improvement regardless of application of unpleasant green slime. Tell Agnes drastic measures are called for as time is running out. Both scour magazines in search of further remedies, all to no avail.

Despatch Agnes to the chemist telling her to ask the apothecary for suitable creams or potions to alleviate said wrinkles. On no account I tell her, is she to charge it to me - I insist she tells him it is for her own personal use. She pulls a face when I suggest she point out her crow's feet. They appear more like scowl lines when she shoots me a disparaging look.

June 10th

After applying lotion to complexion it has turned livid red. The apothecary is a charlatan.

June 11th

Skin is less enraged but is now blotched and dry. Georgie makes sympathetic noises then undoes kind comments by saying have I tried lanolin and lemon which apparently Mama swears by?

June 12th

Panic sets in as skin erupts in pimples. 'Surprise' party will have to be cancelled at this rate as not fit to be seen in public. Furthermore, Spencer adds to my distress by saying the 'rash' is like something he once had after a particularly bad shave.

Burst into tears and retire with large box of chocolates and a decanter of crusted port.

June 13th

Wake to find skin much improved and weather glorious.

Invite select friends to impromptu alfresco luncheon by the river tomorrow. Ask Cook to provide baskets of food and request strawberries and raspberries be incorporated into menu as we have abundance of both here at Upshot Hall. Darling Daughter Clemmie and Spencer Jnr over indulged on them whilst out walking, Miss Grimes informs me when both offspring appear off colour.

Pray the weather stays warm and dry for the morrow.

June 14th

On rising am annoyed to see large grey clouds looming on the horizon. Make alternative plans with Housekeeper in case it should come on to rain which does not please her. Anyone would think I had asked her to stage a full blown dinner at a moment's notice, not move a light luncheon from outside to in, if and when the need arises.

11am - Ask that al fresco luncheon be set up by river as planned when clouds disperse. Need not have worried - it will be fine after all. Anticipated outdoor eating will be great success. The River Nidd, which flows through our estate, will be spectacular backdrop to impromptu party.

At midday - Tell Housekeeper to set up luncheon in the conservatory when rain clouds look imminent.

1pm - Pleased with decision as a few drops of rain fall.

2 pm - Sky clears and the sun spreads its warmth all about making the parkland appear verdant. Instruct

Housekeeper to return luncheon to riverside.

2.30 pm - Guests arrive but notice earlier gentle breeze has turned brisk.

3 pm - In an irate aside Beloved Husband asks what was I thinking of, inviting guests to sit in gale force wind that is whipping off the river. Through gritted teeth tell him there was only a hint of a breeze an hour ago. Heated debate ensues when Spencer says he is certain it will rain.

3.15 pm - Make our way to the riverbank which has been strewn with colourful blankets and shawls - these now weighted down with rocks. Footmen have also thought to bring down chairs for those guests of a less nimble disposition. Guests stand about dithering until luncheon served. Food perfectly adequate but note absence of strawberries and raspberries which had been especially requested.

5 pm - Sun blazes down turning everyone lethargic. Much champagne is drunk in order to stay cool and refreshed. Spencer and William, who had disappeared, arrive back with baskets of strawberries and raspberries. Thank BH effusively for saving the day.

June 15th

Georgie found in the garden, unchaperoned, with Mrs Flight's Charming Brother Simon. Did I not say he was a rakehell? Georgie insists nothing untoward happened and that she was just showing him how she can load a bow. At least the archery instructor was present so in theory she was not alone. To my mind the man is a with chancer - Charming Brother Simon not the archery instructor.

Note: Speak to Miss Trim.

Later explain to Georgie, not for the first time, that as the daughter of an ancient family it is her due to be a credit to our name. It is not enough to be pretty and vivacious; she must endeavour to be above reproach if she is to make a favourable match. She looks suitably contrite but fear this is only so I will leave her be. Go on to say if she is not careful she will fall into an obligation from which she is unable to escape.

Realise my warning has fallen on deaf ears when I hear raucous laughter coming from the garden and see Georgie playing hoopla with a footman.

June 16th

Ask Spencer to have stern word with Georgie regarding her conduct around servants; she might just listen to Beloved Husband, who knows? Both Dear Hattie and I have tried to speak to her I explain, but she takes absolutely no notice whatsoever. Suggest he says he will send her back to Mama if she fails to conform. BH says he will speak to her but cannot spare the time today as he has 'important meeting' with his steward. Strongly suspect Spencer of evasiveness but am pacified when he says he will speak with her tomorrow. Intend to hold him to the appointment.

June 17th

After we have broken our fast, Spencer surprisingly, and without my having to remind him asks to speak with Georgiana privately. Undaunted my little sister follows him to his study. It puts me in mind of a lamb to the slaughter. Spencer can be quite assertive when the need arises and the need has definitely arisen.

Follow them discreetly but cannot hear clearly through the door. Can just make out Spencer's deep voice saying words like 'unseemly' 'unchaperoned' and 'unacceptable', all words I would hope BH to use to severely reprimand my troublesome sister. *Almost* feel sorry for her.

Some time passes when I can hear nothing at all. Then hear what sounds like sniffling. Is Georgiana bowed and broken? Remorseful? Is she crying? With mixed emotions I press ear closer to the door and distinctly hear Spencer say, 'There, there, I know you are young and in need of stimulation but you cannot carry on in this way. Your reputation is at stake'. To my ears this sounds altogether far too lenient. BH should be threatening to tell Mama and sending her home in no uncertain terms. Cannot believe he is allowing her to wrap him around her little finger.

With great restraint stop self from bursting in and saying she is not to go to my 'surprise' party as she has forfeited the right to be treated as a sensible young lady. Realise Spencer will be cross if I do and so wait impatiently to hear what he has to say. Doors are far too thick to hear more than muffled sounds and can only hear Spencer say, 'I will speak to your sister and we will decide what is best'.

The whole encounter is made even more unsatisfactory when I turn to make my exit only to find Housekeeper standing behind me.

Later I go in search of BH as I had thought, wrongly, he would be keen to tell me the outcome of the interview. When pressed he says Georgiana is aware of her mistakes and is to 'mend her ways' and apologise to Dear Hattie and myself. These are the conditions he has stated if she is to be allowed to attend any social engagements for the duration of her stay!

Spencer thy name is gullible.

Go immediately to Georgiana's room where I find her 'experimenting' with her hair. We have a blazing argument the details of which I cannot relate as I am too, too distressed.

Calm nerves with a little laudanum kept especially for just this sort of emergency.

June 18th

My Birthday! Am utterly grateful complexion has returned to normal - even if that means I have as many laughter lines as before.

In readiness for the celebration Agnes styles my hair so it is a mass of curls piled high on my head and then wraps a silk scarf, which matches my gown, around my head. Go down wearing new peacock blue dress with cross over bodice and short puff sleeves. Decided after much thought against gold creation - Georgiana, on seeing it when I was having the last fitting, made such a rude comment it was enough to put me off the entire ensemble.

Spencer, so handsome in new pale grey with canary yellow waistcoat, takes a good look at my hair grins and says 'tre's modern'. He takes my hand then stands back to look me up and down approvingly. He assures me I am just the same as I was when we married ten years ago. Feel it necessary to point out we were married *eight* years ago but nevertheless am pleased with his attempt at a compliment.

BH then takes blue leather box from the side table, the type of box one would expect to contain a bracelet, and presents it to me with a flourish and wishes me a very happy birthday. Am overcome ... on more than one level, on opening the box to find exquisite diamond bracelet with gold 'S' charm by the clasp. Spencer fastens it, and then plants a kiss on the inside of my wrist in quite seductive way. Am charmed but also somewhat perplexed.

Thanks entirely to Dear Hattie my party is a resounding success. My sister is a splendid hostess, the entire county in evidence am pleased to observe. Not even the sight of Lady V can put a damper on the proceedings. Hugo Bright wickedly suggests the lady, wearing purple watered silk, resembles a bruised plum. What a wit he is.

Surprised to see Gerald *sans sa femme*. He says Mariah sends her apologies but as the baby has 'taken its toll' his wife prefers not to be seen out at the present time. Parliament is on summer recess so he will be about until the autumn he informs me. At clandestine meeting in the ante room leading to the library, the sweet man gives me sapphire earrings to match the necklace he bestowed upon me at Christmas. What a thoughtful a gift, I really don't deserve it.

As always Captain Rainer is splendid in his regimentals. He tells me he is to go on manoeuvres next week for at least three months. He asks if I will miss him. I say that I will. Out in the garden we promenade away from the masses and he presents me with a token of his esteem for my birthday. What a lucky girl I am! This time rubies are the stones of choice. Yet another bracelet. At this rate will have to grow another arm.

Note: See how on occasion holding on to one's virtue can be just as rewarding as throwing it to the wind. Will miss the captain but am consoled with the thought I still have Gerald for amusement.

Dance with all the handsome men and manage to avoid The Old Colonel who says he has 'something special' he wishes to show me ... have thoroughly wonderful evening despite this imminent threat. How well life pans out at times, even if one's complexion is showing a little of the signs of aging.

Relent at the last moment and decide to allow Georgiana to attend 'surprise' party but under the watchful eye of Agnes *and* the ancient companion who Agnes says is 'neither use nor ornament' - another of my maid's amusing little sayings. Being so closely monitored Georgie behaves impeccably and only dances with Spencer, William and

Freddie. Hope she has finally learnt a valuable lesson and is now able to take counsel from her elders and betters.

June 19th

Both Spencer and I fail to make an appearance until late afternoon - as Georgie would say we are 'fagged to death' - and only then to partake of a light meal.

Spencer flatters me by saying how beautiful I was last night and then goes on to tell me he loves me more as each year passes. Am quite overcome with his little speech and for once do not suspect he has an ulterior motive. Marital harmony is a welcome visitor at Upshot Hall. Long may it last.

Georgie, not such a welcome guest, behaves in far too loud a manner and when I finally snap, her reply is far too frank for a lady.

Query: At her age was I so self assured and opinionated? I like to think not. When Spencer asks her to desist she rushes from the room and collides with the footman who is just too slow in opening the door to allow her to pass so she slams it closed behind her in dramatic fashion. Realise some lessons have yet to be learnt. Spencer says nothing but then, joy of joys, some little time later he decides to write to Mama regarding the date for Georgiana's departure. At last!

June 20th

Georgie, sensing defeat, is contrite and amenable. Indeed she is a different girl and when Treasured Spinster Friend makes morning call Georgie makes concerted effort to be pleasant to her. She even goes so far as to compliment TSF's hair which we all know is a step too far as TSF has ridden here in the rain. Still, my little sister is trying her best.

June 21st

Much worried when checking Housekeeper's account book to see it inexplicably shows deficit of sixteen pounds nineteen shillings and five pence. Cannot make it balance no matter how hard I try. Fail to understand this as was convinced I had credit balance of eight pounds six shillings and seven pence. Disappointed to find that contents of cash box and accounts do not tally either.

Mem: Ask Georgie, whom I saw by cash box only yesterday, where she got the money from to buy new ribbons.

June 22nd

Begin preparations for walking holiday in The Lakes. Suggest to Housekeeper she organise extra cleaning whilst we are away. She replies, tersely, that Upshot Hall is not in need of extra cleaning but she will do as I ask. Wish I could believe her on both counts.

June 23rd

Spencer asks if arrangements for Spencer Jnr's departure for Eton in the autumn are in hand. Suppress sigh and say of course: new trunks ordered, uniform fitting booked and recommended reading books purchased. Beloved Husband then says he supposes it is too late now to defer son's departure for a year or two. Agree it probably is but say as uniform not yet ordered I suppose we could put off for a year if only to save on the expense. Spencer nods judiciously then suggests we might hire a tutor as compromise. We agree this would be a wise move. BH says I should place advertisement to that effect.

As BH leaves to tell eldest son the good news, the problem of how best to go about hiring competent tutor is uppermost in my thoughts. Decide to ask William for advice. Remember his younger brother had good man prior to him going away to school.

Query: Are mine and Spencer's soft hearts to be applauded? Are we doing the right thing by the boy in not sending him away to school this year?

Answer: Only time will tell.

June 24th

William says his brother's last teacher is older than Methuselah but knows of a tutor who would fit the bill. Agree to see the man with view to hiring him.

June 25th

Pleasant young man bearing the name of Goode is shown into the morning room. Had not expected him so soon, or to be so young, or so good looking.

Luckily had compiled a list of suitable enquires and was

pleased when he answered them all with flying colours. Hired him on the spot as he was recommended by brother-in-law. He is to begin teaching Spencer Jnr in late August. Pray Georgie will have gone home by then as guess she will suddenly take an interest in all things academic if she claps eyes on handsome Mr Goode.

June 26th

When mention to eldest son have appointed a tutor he receives the good news by stuffing the last of the cake he is demolishing into his mouth. Fear the guineas we save on school fees will not be offset with the food bill to feed Spencer Jnr as he has the most voracious appetite for a boy his age.

Query: Why is sherry decanter in the library perpetually empty?

Note: Ask Blake to look into the matter.

The butler will get to the bottom of this problem I am certain. Unlike some of the servants, Blake can always be relied upon. Would like to reward him for his loyalty but we both realise the paying of higher wages would be offensive to us both.

June 27th

Spencer says Mama has replied to his letter begging him to keep Georgiana a little longer as she is laid low with a summer cold. Ask him if he believes this story - not for one moment do I - he says nothing then shrugs in resigned manner. In fairness he offers that Georgie is behaving remarkably well of late. Indeed she is being helpful, amusing and polite am forced to agree. Spencer of course takes all the credit for this and says it is as a result of his 'timely intervention'.

Decide a reward is due to my younger sister and so treat Georgie by allowing her to accompany me to Harrogate to help choose items for my walking holiday.

Bump into an acquaintance of Dear Hattie's, an Artistic Type named Harris Waverly. I think I am right in saying he is a painter of some renown. Am about to invite him to take tea at Moorlands when Treasured Spinster Friend appears as if from nowhere (navy blue day dress with a bodice that appears a little tight to my eye). Am forced to include her in the invitation or it will look churlish in the extreme.

At Moorlands - Dear Hattie as always most generous in allowing us to use her house as our own - Georgie behaves herself which is more than can be said of TSF. Anyone would think she has never met a good looking gentleman before. She has long (tedious) conversation with him regarding her own 'artistic endeavours' and he, being a polite young man, offers her tips and guidance. When Georgie offers to show him the family portraits, am most relieved. Fear TSF came across as quite the desperate spinster. Even Georgie noticed and said TSF was 'dangling after' Mr Waverly in most obvious way. For once Georgie and I are in complete agreement.

June 28th

Back at Upshot Georgie's archery instructor says she is an exceptional student. Admit to Spencer I am more than a little astounded.

June 29th

Treasured Spinster Friend calls to tell me Harris Waverly is to give her painting lessons. See how she is now resorting to such levels of desperation in order to entrap a man. How excruciatingly embarrassing for all concerned.

June 30th

Feel I should give Georgie the benefit of my experience and help her to learn how to be able to converse intelligently on a wide variety of subjects of general interest. This I think will help her to secure regard not only of gentlemen, but also of ladies. Hitherto she appears preoccupied with conversing *only* with gentlemen and only bothering to speak to ladies when the men are absent. Tell her she must strive to make herself agreeable to both sexes. Say how she should take an interest in the lives of her female acquaintances, offer compliments or ask after their families. Also suggest that to be pleasing company she should be well informed and keep abreast of what is happening in the world. To this end supply her with The Times and say we will discuss current affairs when she has read it.

After luncheon ask Georgiana what she has learnt from The Times. She frowns and looks as if she would rather have a tooth pulled then says the Prime Minister sounds like a fool and why anyone would listen to him is beyond her. Point out, patiently, that the quickest way to ruin a pleasant conversation in company is to talk about politics or religion. She throws her hands in the air in most irate manner and asks why did I not tell her this before as she has just wasted all morning reading about political crisis. Point out I said 'subjects of general interest' by which I meant not politics and not religion. Suggest Georgie try again but can see her attention span, never long in the first place, has wavered. Decide to leave further instruction for another day.

Note: Suggest in next letter to Mama that she should pay more attention to this aspect of Georgiana's upbringing; my little sister comes across as quite unpolished because she has a narrow view of the world. Still, she is not yet sixteen and has much to learn. No doubt at her age I too came across as gauche, yet I know for a fact I made an effort to include ladies in my circle of acquaintances. Georgie should model herself upon Dear Hattie and myself then she will not go far wrong.

July

July 1st

Persistent rain keeps us indoors all day. Georgie and I endeavour to teach Darling Daughter Clemmie the steps to the latest dances but we both fear she has two left feet. Lank hair and an inability to dance elegantly will not a bride make.

July 2nd

Call to see Treasured Spinster Friend and am shown into the garden where Harris Waverly is tutoring her in the finer points of flower painting. She is fussing and batting her eyelashes in a most alarming way, I fear she will take flight. Am there a full fifteen minutes before she even thinks to offer tea.

Harris is a studious young man and whilst we partake of tea he is busy at his sketch book. When I ask to see what he has drawn I blush to see it is a pencil sketch of myself. How flattering. He offers it to me as a little reminder of our time together.

TSF glares at me suspiciously but what can I say? Is it my fault I have good bones? Think perhaps it is time to have a quiet word with my closest and oldest friend. Suggest she tries not to be quite so obvious in her manner where single gentlemen are concerned. Most bachelors are put off by her over-effusive demeanour I fear; have noticed she can appear quite unsophisticated in eligible male company.

July 3rd

Glorious change in the weather. Carry painting materials to garden with intention of continuing self improvement by undertaking water colour of rose arbour with basket of roses artfully placed on the seat. Set up easel ready to begin when Lady V is announced. Does the lady have no one else to visit?

Of course she immediately asks if she may suggest the basket also contain maidenhair ferns and some forget-me-nots which, she is certain, will give ethereal look to the composition. Bite lip and say I really want Rosa Banksiae to be star attraction of arrangement. Undeterred she calls over to Brown and asks him to procure said ferns and flowers. Head Gardener, quite rightly, checks with me before presenting her with the specimens which she then adds to the basket.

Order lemonade which we take in the shade of the arbour (which I am supposed to be recording for posterity) and talk about the Dutch school of painting, the importance of pruning clematis at the correct time of year and the Lake District. Lady V insists the Lakes should only be visited in early spring so one can appreciate the azaleas. Tell her we are going next week and that Spencer has horror of azaleas - untrue as I doubt he would recognise one if he saw one.

Lady V says we must be sure to call at the most northern Lakes as these far superior to more southern ones. Decline to tell her our itinerary is set and hint heavily that the best of the sun will soon be gone from this part of the garden. Eventually she says how naughty I am to keep her talking and now she will be late for her next appointment.

Query: Why do I always feel impelled to lie to Lady V? There must be some flaw in my character which makes me feel the need to tell falsehoods in her presence. Will endeavour to stay quiet in future rather than tell untruths.

Begin preliminary sketch of arbour. Housekeeper comes and asks for permission to order new sink for laundry room as old one has cracked and now leaks. Give permission and return attention to sketch. Spencer then creeps up behind me causing me to drop my pencil, and says have I seen his form book as he and Freddie are to go to York to the races. Ask him why on earth I should know where it is as do not even know of its existence. Georgie arrives and asks will Spencer put ten shillings on Golden Flame for her. This suggests to both of us that Georgiana might know the whereabouts of said book. Spencer marches Georgiana into the house muttering ominously, leaving me wondering from where she got ten shillings.

Footman arrives and says luncheon is served, after which large rain clouds appear. Am forced to tell servants to bring in painting paraphernalia.

Query: How is mind to be broadened when mundane

matters of domesticity intrude upon one's day to such an extent? Was the 'Literary Lioness' so plagued one wonders, and if so am surprised she ever wrote more than a prologue. Am not surprised it is rumoured she is a spinster, were she a married lady with a house and family she would not have the time to scribble even a note to her dressmaker.

Rain hurls itself against the windows as I search in vain for Mansfield Park. As it is now just the sort of day to curl up with a book, send to the summerhouse where am convinced I left it. Eventually it is run to ground in the library in sister's sticky fingers - she is once again eating cake. The girl has even more of an appetite than Dear Hattie and Spencer Jnr combined.

Georgie declares Mansfield Park to be most boring book ever written. I say she will not mind then if I have it back as she continues to chew enormous slice of fruit cake, before flouncing out in attitude of unquiet rebellion and knocking over an arrangement of Peonies. Notice when she has gone the sherry decanter is empty.

Ask Blake when he last filled it and am told it was replenished that very morning.

July 4th

Write to Mama saying Spencer insists Georgiana return home immediately. Know full well am wasting paper and ink but as Spencer now totally convinced of Georgiana's transformation into pleasant young lady know he has given up petitioning Mama.

July 5th

After excellent dinner at the Pascoes, discover Georgiana in the garden with good looking young officer. Separate her forcibly from Captain Wilkes. Unpleasant scene then ensues when I point out she is risking her reputation (again) to be seen with a gentleman and without her chaperone in attendance. More flouncing and sulking from younger sister. - Miss Trim is later caught napping in the conservatory.

Note: Have words with Georgie's maid - again.

Dear Hattie (such a support) takes Georgie aside and tries her best to remonstrate with her but the girl is beyond unreasonable. Georgie's temper flares up alarmingly quickly which means she is in a vile and uncompromising mood. Had thought after Spencer's 'timely intervention' she had turned a corner - it appears not.

Am forced to actually leave the party early and escort her back to Upshot Hall - cannot rely upon Miss Trim to get her home safely - endure Georgie's wrath all the way to her bedroom where I lock her in. Feel this is over reaction but the girl simply cannot be trusted. Lately have turned a blind eye when she has spent far too much time flirting with the footmen - think how she has to have some fun. Was appalled to learn from Agnes Georgiana's latest pastime is baiting the young servants to fight each other - bad enough, but then to be taking side bets on the winner is beyond the pale.

Later when Spencer arrives home, says the girl is 'way too headstrong' and if Dear Daughter Clementine takes after her Aunt Georgiana he will be forced to send her to a convent.

Note: Write to Mama in the morning saying Georgiana will be sent home on the morrow come what may and whether she is there to receive her or not. Furthermore, strongly suggest she replace Miss Trim with younger, more alert maid. Miss Trim, who must be fifty if she is a day, cannot keep up with Georgie and her escapades.

July 6th

Georgiana has run away. Or at least we thought she had but it transpires she had merely been skulking in the orangery. She climbed out of her bedroom window - one has to hand it to the girl she does not let a mere locked door stand in her way. When found she is given stern lecture by Spencer, who says her antics will no longer be tolerated. He gives instructions that her trunks be packed and says she should be ready to leave in two hours. Am so pleased with Beloved Husband's manly show of strength. Who knew he had it in him? Not I for one and not Georgiana for another.

In no uncertain terms and not cowed *at all* Georgiana tells Spencer she never thought him to be so 'hateful and unfeeling'. At once he seeks to pacify her. Fear she will again talk her way out of the situation. But then she says Dear Hattie and I are no better than Mama; we are mean and matronly. MATRONLY! Under the circumstances Spencer is driven to rebuke her most forcefully. Georgiana then throws all sense of decorum out of the window and rants and raves and generally behaves in a most unbecoming manner. Her complexion turns quite red but she is not done yet. She then attempts to throw me, her Devoted Sister who has given her shelter these last weeks, under the carriage. Before heading for the door she adds caustically, 'by the way brother-in-law do you realise SHE is playing you false?' My sister then points her finger at ME in over dramatic gesture that would look well on stage at Covent Garden. Briefly consider slapping the girl. My temper is finally well and truly lost. When she flounces out the door rattles as she slams it shut behind her in histrionic gesture.

Spencer, his composure remarkably intact, follows her out into the hall and tells her, as she runs up the stairs, that she will find herself unmarriageable if she carries on behaving in this manner. Am most shocked by his rebuke in the hearing of the Housekeeper who is passing through the hall at the time. However, Georgiana it appears is not at all cowed or embarrassed. Her bedroom door is once again loosened from its hinges as she bangs it closed behind her.

We hear the sound of sobbing from within. Spencer cautions me to leave her be when I try to follow, saying 'enough is enough'. This is a whole new side to my Beloved Husband and frankly one I am mesmerised by.

Georgiana is last seen making rude gesture through the carriage window to no one in particular as she finally leaves Upshot Hall for home.

July 7th

Upshot feels suddenly restored to normality now Georgiana has left us. Of course I am fond of my little sister, but keeping track of her is most straining on the nerves. The sooner Mama finds her a husband the better.

Agnes says my unworn white and gold ensemble (the one I was going to wear for my 'surprise' birthday party and the one Georgie was so rude about), has 'gone'. We both know to where it has gone and with whom.

Peaceful half hour spent with Mansfield Park before Spencer startles me by asking what Georgiana meant by suggesting I was playing him false. Say I have no idea and that the girl barely made sense her wrath was so great. Also add how well he handled the affair with my ungrateful little sister and say that Darling Daughter Clemmie is in safe hands with him to watch over her. Suggest early night in way of reward. Spencer and I behave like newlyweds for some time after Georgie's departure.

July 8th

Beloved Husband arrives in my bed chamber with a large, beribboned box of my favourite truffles. What a sweet man I married.

Decide to bring forward our Lake sojourn now Georgie has left us.

Cook serves possibly the worst meal I have ever had the misfortune to eat.

Final preparations for Lake Tour. Spencer tells me he

intends to climb and walk every mountain he sees. I say happily I will accompany him.

July 9th

Much to be done today all of which takes time and effort to organise but am a great one for delegating. Supervising packing, leaving instructions for the Housekeeper, and making sure the Dear Children will be settled sends maids skittering about the house in a frenzy of activity. I barely have a moment to myself such is the commotion.

Consider fitting in short ride on the moors to say a fond farewell to Gerald but decide against the plan and spend the time with my handsome Beloved Husband instead. He really is so devoted to me.

July 10th

Dear Hattie and William call for us in their carriage (which is bigger than ours and far better sprung). William's coat of arms is striking and recognisable by all, being painted in gold on the dark blue carriage doors.

We chat animatedly about which lakes and peaks we are looking forward to conquering - our guide book tells us there are no actual mountains in the Lake District but this does not dampen our enthusiasm. En route pass three peaks called Ingleborough, Penyghent and another one whose name escapes me. The weather is bright and cheerful - as are we.

Our first night is spent at Jackson Hall in a pretty little town called Kirkby Lonsdale. From the three storey building, which is well situated overlooking the market square, we take a pre-prandial stroll by the river with spectacular views over pastureland. Am charmed by all I see. Dinner is better than anticipated and when Dear Hattie says she would not be at all unhappy to dine so well for the whole sojourn we all agree wholeheartedly. We retire early replete and merry.

July 11th

Glorious summer sunshine to start the day. After breaking our fast early we continue our journey to Windermere which is to be our first lake. Dear Hattie and I peer excitedly through the carriage window hoping to catch a glimpse of the lake. Arrive at the inn where we are to stay and are happy it is well appointed and has views of the lake from every window. Bowness-on-Windermere we all agree is spectacular.

Wearing new olive green walking dress and jacket we venture on a boat trip after late luncheon. Sadly we note the food not as good as Jackson Hall.

Dear Hattie very ill on the boat.

Note: Condition cannot be seasickness as we are not at sea and the lake is not at all choppy. Was it is something she ate? As we all partook of the same food this is most unlikely. Tell self not to worry about DH, she is generally healthy and of a robust constitution. Feel sure she will soon be restored to full health.

July 12th

Windermere. Cloudy but atmospheric weather. We are late setting out as Dear Hattie still unaccountably unwell. Today we are to walk around the southern end of the lake (sage green pelisse with straw hat with little feather at jaunty angle). Am cross when new sturdy walking boots pinch somewhat after just a ten minutes stroll.

We had planned to sail back on the ferryboat but as DH is still a little green about the gills it is agreed William and Spencer will follow the plan and I will take the carriage back with DH. Am much relieved as new walking boots have rubbed painful blisters on each heel.

Query: How can something so small and innocuous looking cause pain which is more agonising than childbed labour? Doubt I shall be able to walk anywhere tomorrow.

Dine much later than DH and I would have liked as Spencer and William decide to get lost on the way back to the hotel. Thanks to the hospitality of our host we miss them hardly at all. As torrential rain sets in a planned evening stroll is cancelled.

By bedtime DH is a little better. The fine wine is no doubt an excellent restorative.

July 13th

Cloudy and unseasonably chilly. DH once more incapacitated so spend the morning shopping whilst Spencer and William hire a guide to take them up one of the steeper, more rugged climbs. DH joins us for luncheon but hardly eats a thing. Cannot ever recall her toying with her food in such an uninterested manner. Admit I am quite worried about her.

Slight drizzle begins to descend as we set off on our next adventure; an afternoon spent walking by the northern end of Bowness-on-Windermere - stunning views across the lake towards the hills.

Note: Must capture one of the lakes in watercolour, preferably on a dry day.

We cheerfully climb a craggy path a little above the lake so we can fully appreciate the view from above. As Wordsworth points out it is easy to immerse oneself in such spectacular scenery. Spencer says the hill is hardly an incline at all and nothing like as steep as the one he and William attempted the day before. Definitely feel warm as we ascend and am aware of muscles straining in most disconcerting manner.

After a quarter of an hour DH asks whether the climb flattens out soon. After consulting his guide book William tells her he is certain it does. Our path is then hindered by rocks and boulders which need to be clambered over in most unladylike fashion. Say light heartedly what fun this is then tear new jacket sleeve as I slide off large jagged rock scuffing new footwear.

After two hours we reach the top of the peak, which does indeed feel like a mountain. Turn to fully appreciate the glorious view (as promised by husbands) but entire lake is obscured from sight by thick fog. Descent hampered by heavy rain. Who would have believed the path would become a mud bath so soon? Gloom descends.

Pray Italian Lakes may be affordable next year.

July 14th

Leave Windermere and head north to Keswick. Our new (superior) guidebook -purchased in a quaint little book shop - tells us Scafell Pike is the highest point. Contrary to earlier information Scafell Pike *is* a mountain; in fact it is the highest mountain in England at an elevation of 3208 feet.

Note: On returning to Yorkshire write to publisher of (inferior) guidebook and say the publication is misleading at best and incorrect at worst.

Arrive at the Lodore Falls Hotel where Dear Hattie and I especially wanted to stay as the guidebook (the new superior one) says there is a pretty waterfall to explore close by.

Before dinner and after poring over the map for an hour, William and Spencer engage a guide to take us up Scafell Pike. Now we have seen it (it truly is a mountain) DH and I share reservations about our abilities to reach the top. We are assured by guide (ruggedly handsome DH and I note) that we will be perfectly capable of the ascent. How he can tell from simply looking at us am unsure but feel quite bolstered by his confidence in us. Am sure in his safe, manly hands we will bound to the summit like mountain goats.

July 15th

Keswick. The sun shines and there is not a cloud to be seen in the sky as we set off on our expedition to walk to Scafell Pike. Meet our guide who asks Dear Hattie and I whether we should not wear bonnets. We had decided, together, that bonnets would be an encumbrance and say so. 'That's the spirit', says our guide as he strides ahead. We set off full of excitement, anticipation and enthusiasm.

The first part of the walk is a pleasant stroll through a wooded area at the bottom of the pike. Our guide, thoughtfully, has us stop and listen to various birdsong and points out red squirrels which can be seen clambering up tall trees. DH and I in particular are thrilled with the nature we are witnessing first hand. The squirrels are altogether bigger and more robust than the ones in our own parkland.

Coming out of the wood the path becomes a little steeper and the sun, now high in the sky, scorches the back of our necks. Husbands are forced to lend us their handkerchiefs as there is no shade to be had WHATSOEVER.

After what feels like hours (could have sworn that around the next bend we would have reached the summit) we come upon a large boulder. Guide suggests we rest and take light refreshments, which he has thoughtfully brought in something called a knapsack. Our Guide we note is barely out of breath, whereas DH and myself struggle for air. If my face is the same colour as DH's Agnes will be able to see me from our hotel.

Guide provides us with rustic fare and a bottle of water.

Spencer most unimpressed with liquid refreshment on offer. I, on the other hand, peer longingly at the lake and wish I could throw myself in even though I cannot swim. The last time I was this hot was visiting Aged Aunt. Top lip is definitely glistening.

The next stage of the climb is a 'little steeper' our guide informs us considerately. He asks would we ladies like to rest here rather than overtire ourselves? Do not want to lose his confidence so assure him we are stronger than we look and would not dream of being left behind.

With hindsight recollect how it is DH who makes this brave assertion.

More painful blisters erupt and a slip means I graze a knee but eventually reach the top of Scafell Pike. The view is, as we were promised, truly magnificent. What an achievement! Will certainly be extolling the virtues of mountain climbing to all who will listen on return home. Try, in vain, to bring to mind Wordsworth's poetic words.

Sadly DH is violently ill behind a boulder.

The descent, worryingly, is almost as perilous as the ascent, and takes just as long to get down as it did to climb up. DH leans heavily upon our guide all the way as William and Spencer race ahead like school boys completely unaware of DH's plight. We are both in agreement their behaviour is most ungentlemanly. We say this out of earshot of our guide of course when he kindly pushes a boulder the size of a horse out of our path.

Back at our hotel tell Agnes I will soak in a bath and

take dinner in my room. Cannot ever recall feeling so exhausted. Fall asleep before dinner arrives and do not wake until after eleven the next morning.

July 16th

Husbands suggest a relaxing day admiring the Lodore Falls - Spencer has a headache, presumably got from too much sun the day before. DH and I happily agree to a more sedate schedule, after all the falls are but a mere stroll from the hotel our new guidebook informs us. We order hampers to take with us which we all agree will be most diverting.

As I am dressing (heather and green checked day dress with pretty little hat with pheasant feather) Agnes relays that a maid at the hotel says we should take the carriage to the falls. Her informer says it is 'quite a trek' for ladies.

Go to DH's room and am shocked to discover she is still pale and drawn. Encourage her to take a drop or two of laudanum. She assures me she is well despite my fears but manages to partake nonetheless. Together we decide to err on the side of caution and order the carriage for two o' clock. We compare blisters and agree our feet will never be the same again.

William scorns the idea of taking the carriage and suggests a brisk walk is just the thing he and husband need to clear their heads - Spencer is uncertain but agrees.

Also staying at our hotel are several experienced gentlemen walkers and climbers whom our husbands have befriended with alacrity. William and Spencer have found the like- minded young gentlemen both entertaining and informative. After dinner they all compare notes about their day's 'hikes'. This involves copious amounts of bragging - mainly from Spencer and William it has to be said. The evenings generally end with tales of their exploits - greatly exaggerated - and them all drinking far too much and gambling late into the night. Not wishing to let William down, the pair set off to walk to the falls a little after midday, Spencer looking slightly jaundiced. Last night a wager was taken involving climbing an outside wall - astonishingly Spencer won the bet but is now paying the price as he strained something in the process.

DH (light blue and cream check day dress) and I fortify ourselves with luncheon and rather excellent claret, and then board the carriage. So grateful Agnes warned us about the distance to the waterfall; it is indeed *miles* away from our hotel. We are deposited by the river but still cannot see the falls. The groom says it is not possible to get nearer as the track is too narrow and so we set up 'base camp' and wait for William and Spencer, who we are surprised to find, are not here already. Could have sworn they would arrive before us.

It begins to drizzle.

An hour passes. After a little sustenance we set off with a groom as guide. The sky is turning dark and ominous as we come upon the waterfall. It is not as spectacular as we had been led to believe, barely a trickle really. We have bigger cascades at Upshot Hall although ours of course, are manmade. Would have been quite livid had we decided to walk all the way.

Note: Another remark to the publisher of the (new) guidebook methinks!

Arrive back at the carriage to see husbands tucking into food as if they have not fed for a week. They decide to give the Lodore Falls a miss when we say they are not so very big or impressive. We all travel back in the carriage as hail lashes the windows and thunder and lightning reverberates from the hills, peaks, pikes and mountains.

No doubt the waterfall will be positively gushing now.

Before dinner DH and I compare aches and pains of which we have many. Both agree we never imagined walking could be so painful. Generally it is not a topic we ladies give much thought to. Limbs are heavy and quite beyond even the slightest movement. Feel sure if we carry on with this madness we shall both have muscles like the strong men at fairground attractions.

Dinner is a sombre affair as we can barely stay awake. When we leave the gentlemen to take their port DH says she is convinced she has sprained something vital and hitches her skirt to reveal a bruise the size and colour of a large plum - She then blocks all heat from the fire as she warms her behind but I do not have the heart, or the energy, to chastise her.

Am so ravenously hungry eat all the biscuits washed down by a good burgundy. This in itself is most unusual as

DH, despite all the fresh air, still has the appetite of a bird. She tentatively suggests a later start tomorrow to give us a little more time to recover ourselves.

When Spencer and William join us, put this proposal to them and they agree we ought to set off after luncheon as it is not too far to the next lake. At this point none of us can remember for which lake we are bound.

The gentlemen then propose they will play cards with their new friends. DH and I decide to leave them to it - they are making their way down the brandy decanter at a fair pace - and retire early. On the landing tentatively broach the subject which has been at the forefront of my mind all evening.

Suggest hesitantly that tomorrow we could go home.

DH is about to remonstrate when she then thinks of her own feather bed and linen sheets - she actually says this out loud in a dreamy, coveting voice. Together we agree our feet and aching limbs are not up to the rigours of mountaineering. Will not of course share these thoughts with Lady V under ANY circumstances.

Later when I tell Spencer DH and I are to return home he says nothing and instantly falls asleep again.

July 17th

Over breakfast The Duke says he and Spencer will of course continue on as planned. Spencer agrees muttering he will stay with William as he does not want to leave him alone and it would be a shame to miss seeing Skiddaw and

Derwentwater.

DH and I, already packed, prepare to set off for the comforts of home. Spencer bids me a fond farewell as if he may never see me again; am touched by his affection. Press upon BH how he should take care on the mountains as, despite what Georgiana thinks about widows, I do not want to be one quite yet.

July 18th

Break our journey once again at Kirkby Lonsdale and enjoy a peaceful evening in the company of other weary travellers. Retire early so that we may make an early start on the morrow.

July 19th

Upshot Hall. Am always astounded at the accrual of domestic catastrophes that awaits one after even the briefest absence. The Cook has given notice and two upstairs maids have left - left already without giving notice! Servants today have no sense of loyalty whatsoever. The Housekeeper asks how she is to recruit more servants when existing staff still not paid this quarter's wages. Want to say 'how should I know?' but cannot antagonise the woman further or she too will threaten to leave my employ.

Was there ever a lady so tried as I?

Fraught interview with Cook who insists she cannot be prevailed upon to stay *this* time as she has another place 'lined up'. Offer to raise her salary. She says I still owe her last quarter's pay. Had anticipated some vulgar toing and froing about money so had earlier found several guineas in Spencer's 'secret' hiding place - the back of the bottom drawer of his desk in the study.

Cook and I finally reach an accommodation but she says if pay not forthcoming next quarter she will indeed be forced to leave. Feel justifiably irate at being blackmailed by the detestable woman but what can one say under the circumstances? I blame Spencer.

Note: If we should ever be in a position of solvency, shall take great pleasure in dismissing the wretched woman.

Housekeeper then informs me there has been a leak in the east wing due to a hole in the roof and should she instruct someone to mend it? Bite back cutting remark and ask her to deal with the matter forthwith.

Query: Must I do everything myself around here?

Darling Daughter Clemmie has a cold. Spencer Jnr with total disdain and lack of feeling for his sister says she is keeping him awake with her coughing. Instruct nursemaid to move DDC to another bedroom. Why Miss Grimes could not think of this solution unaided is beyond reason. I am to be nursemaid as well as housekeeper! Spend the afternoon with a sherry and feet in a footbath. Dear Hattie sends note and begs me to dine with her, of course am only too happy to oblige. After a good dinner at which DH and I rather over indulge - she would insist on champagne before, during and after dinner - she tells me she is almost certain she is to expect a happy event.

What wonderful news. Am so thrilled for her.

The Duke has not yet been informed she adds (she thinks not to raise his hopes just in case she is mistaken), a sentiment I think most wise.

This then explains her loss of appetite - which now thankfully is restored.

We spend a happy hour trying on names for the baby - I strive and am successful in persuading her Fanny is not dignified name for the daughter of a duke. If it is a boy undoubtedly he will be named after William so do not even bother to think of names for a boy child. I rather like Alicia but decline from putting this name forward in case I should have another girl - I should very much like another daughter. DH says she likes Jane - Plain Jane! Suggest Anne but DH says she was at the ladies seminary with an 'Anne' and she cannot agree to the name as the Anne in question had an unfortunate condition. Apparently she had odd coloured eyes! How we laugh until DH becomes morbidly superstitious and says we should not mock the afflicted - this in case *her* progeny is born with some such defect. Say how could any child of The Duke's be anything less than perfect but DH is determined not to tempt fate.

Stay the night at DH's as by the time we finish choosing names - both agree Charlotte is far too common but Marianne is perfect - it is almost dawn. Once abed we again compare bruises. DH's, am reluctant to admit, are much more impressive than my own. Feel somewhat put out about this as my limbs ache every bit as badly as hers yet I have nothing much to show for it. Show her the scab on my right knee which is the best I can do.

July 20th

To clear our heads in the morning we venture out in the carriage (our feet still cannot support us for more than a few steps). Pass Lady V's carriage and both groan as now she knows we are back from our Lake Adventure she will surely call on one or other of us.

Back at High Brow House Dear Hattie instructs servants we are not at home to visitors.

July 21st

Lady V arrives at Upshot shortly after midday to make a morning call. She enquires (rudely in my humble opinion) why I am returned early from my sojourn. Once again am reduced to lying. Say (unconvincingly) Dear Hattie and I only ever intended to do the first part of the Lake Adventure as we had pressing engagements here at home. Thankfully she is so self absorbed she does not ask what these are and so I am saved from telling more untruths.

Do I realise, she says, ladies today take extensive walking holidays in Italy for pleasure? I say I can well believe it as DH and I were captivated by 'hiking' and intend to tour the Italian Lakes next year. Lady V declares she too is to travel to Lake Garda in the spring where she will stay with her 'good friend' Count G.

Query: Could this be the same Count G with whom I had a *liaison* many moons ago?

Did I not find the air invigorating asks Lady V scrutinising my face to see if complexion has suffered from the exposure. Am sure she has noticed the effects of sun as freckles have made unwelcome appearance. As always am left feeling exceedingly irritated by Lady V's visit and am glad when she leaves.

July 22nd

Agnes applies preparation to face in an attempt to fade freckles.

July 23rd

Extremely Alarming News - Missive from Mother-in-Law saying she is to pay us a visit. Several scenarios crash through brain, situations which involve the whole family being struck down with infectious disease making it impossible for her to come.

See date she is to arrive; four days hence. There is only one thing worse than visit from MIL and that is a visit in which Beloved Husband is absent. Think to send letter to the lakes but then reconsider; forewarned is forearmed. Would not put it past BH to stay away for another month if he knows his mama is about to descend.

When MIL removed to a house on the Norfolk estate after our wedding I was only relieved she was not living in the same county. She makes a point of 'not interfering', which means she meddles all the time, usually behind my back.

In her opinion, no one else's view matters it seems, Upshot Hall is too hot, too cold, too dusty, over staffed, understaffed, in need of modernisation or full of new fangled inventions like running water - the latter according to her being the 'devil's work'.

Ring for Housekeeper to inform her MIL's rooms should be prepared, menus redone and knives kept sharpened in case am pushed beyond endurance, which is usual state of affairs by third day of MIL's visit.

Do not say last point out loud but wonder how to ask Housekeeper to manage this without causing anxiety.

July 24th

Spencer arrives home unannounced and is carried dramatically into the drawing room by two footmen. Fearing he has caught some incurable disease and I will be left a young widow with three children to raise all alone, throw myself at him only to find he has sprained an ankle.

Inform BH his mother is to visit at which news he takes to his bed.

July 25th

Drastic situations require drastic measures. Take the carriage to Harrogate where, after several deep breaths, I enter the most fashionable jewellers on Montpellier Street.

Earlier had selected a piece of jewellery which although

has a sentimental attachment is not a family heirloom. Decided to sell rather than pawn in the hope of receiving a higher price and thereby being able to not only pay Cook last quarter's salary but also pay *all* the main household creditors who continue to clamour at our door. By selling the sapphires Gerald gave to me, hope to be able to get through MIL's visit reasonably sane. Without money to replenish the wine cellar this is inconceivable - wine merchant categorically states he cannot deliver monthly order until debt cleared 'once and for all' - had been trying to pacify him with a little on account but apparently 'this will no longer do'.

Tense, mortifying and altogether shameful discussion with jeweller. Finally resort to dabbing eye with lace handkerchief but even this does not move the man. At last we agree a price (including having paste replica made of the jewels - clever me for thinking of this). In the end receive more for the sapphires than I could ever have imagined, which is a lovely, lovely surprise. Never thought for one moment Gerald held me in so much esteem. Am extremely pleased and quite touched. If only I did not have to part with them but sadly needs must.

On returning home summon Housekeeper and give her the good news; all staff will be remunerated and all merchants paid forthwith.

Tell Spencer we are out of the woods, but do not tell him where the money has come from or indeed that there are funds left over after main debts discharged. Thankfully he has never been overly curious and is too overjoyed to ask for details. Necessity of inventing white lie as to where monies had come from - story of an Aged Uncle who always had a soft spot for me dying and leaving me money in his will - totally uncalled for. BH, ungratefully, says if only Aged Aunt would hurry and shuffle off the mortal coil then we would be *really* rich.

July 26th

Pay call to Dear Hattie to tell her of impending doom. Trying to rally me she says MIL's visit will not be for long. Tell her it will *seem* long.

As today is last day of freedom before MIL arrives, back at Upshot Hall Spencer and I make merry now wine cellar restocked.

July 27th

Spencer welcomes his mama to Upshot Hall with his foot raised on a stool. MIL says she always knew he would succumb to gout; his father was a martyr to the condition she informs us.

He tells her remarkable story of how he came to be injured on a mountain and despite agonising pain assures her he will soon be up and about. Several times over dinner she advises her son to lay off the wine as it will do his gout no good at all. Later as we leave to take tea she forbids him the port bottle.

July 28th

MIL says breakfast (which thankfully she generally takes in her bedchamber) was 'adequate' but might she suggest Cook endeavours to serve it hot in future. Cannot think how am to broach the matter with Cook without her making idle threats. Decide to leave issue alone for now and hope matter resolves itself. Odds are the next meal will at least be lukewarm as Cook is nothing if not inconsistent.

At luncheon MIL pointedly asks if cold fare is a new fashion. Typically Cook could not raise her game to produce tepid repast. Understand difficulty as the kitchen is quite a long way from the dining room but it is hard to see how the problem can be rectified unless we take to eating our meals in the kitchen.

Mem: Put problem of cold fare to Housekeeper - again. When I mention problem she all but shrugs her shoulders in most unhelpful way and says she will 'see what I can do'. This means she will tell Cook who will also shrug and that will be the end of the matter. Sometimes I do not know why I bother.

July 29th

Unexpected arrival of Aged Aunt swathed in enough blankets to furnish six beds. Ask Spencer if he was aware Aged Aunt was to make a visit but he assures me it is as much news to him as it is to me.

MIL welcomes Aged Aunt and orders all fires to be banked up and shawls brought to further entomb Aged Aunt.

Fear we will all pass out from heat exhaustion before supper.

July 30th

Aged Aunt and MIL both complain of temperature of house *and* food.

July 31st

Lady V makes morning call. Oh joy - do I not suffer enough?

She and MIL spend happy hour catching up on news and gossip. Notice how both ladies suddenly appear completely different in each other's company. Spend some moments wondering why this should be and can only assume each is trying to outdo the other.

Lady V says she can see MIL's touch in floral arrangement on a side table. She is indeed correct in her assumption as earlier MIL took it upon herself to arrange a variety of garish flowers gathered for her by Brown. The tasteful one I had placed there only yesterday not in evidence - ANYWHERE.

Aged Aunt makes an appearance and shuffles to sit beside me so that she is closest to the fire, says the place for flowers is either in the garden or at best on a grave (whose she does not say) she then eats her way through the cake with an appetite I have yet to see matched in one so old.

Later, MIL suggests I employ a pastry cook as cakes and pastries were unimaginative and unpalatable - clearly not inedible as Aged Aunt proved.

Dinner given for MIL to reacquaint her with old friends

is almost a disaster when I ask Blake in an aside why Lamb and Beef have not made an appearance. Specifically remember asking Cook to order expensive cuts from the butcher. MIL it transpires has seen fit to change menu to one she thought was 'lighter' and more 'suitable'. Everything is covered in cream which cannot in my book make the food 'lighter' or more 'suitable'. Spencer, oblivious, says jovially how Cook has pulled out all the stops and adds that the food is actually hot for a change. MIL smiles beatifically and says she hopes I do not think she was interfering but she had 'a word' with the Housekeeper. Catch Dear Hattie's eye and she smiles sympathetically. What would I do without my sister?

Congratulate self on remembering to invite Hugo Bright to stay as he, as always, is so much fun and helps me to keep the situation in perspective - and from harming MIL with knives that may well be blunt.

When the gentlemen are at their port and brandy and MIL has gone to powder her nose DH and I giggle like school girls and down brandy as if it is going out of fashion. Aged Aunt I note is able to match us glass for glass until she falls asleep snoring loudly. The rest of the evening passes in a blur.

Mem: Mention to Housekeeper strange smell emanating from morning room.

August

August 1ˢᵗ

MIL is surprise (unwelcome) guest at the breakfast table. Had hoped to enjoy peace and quiet alone for an hour but this clearly was too much to ask. Spencer suffering digestive upset - possibly as a result of last night's rich food.

After scaring the little serving maid half to death by barking order for HOT coffee and HOT eggs MIL addresses me as if I am a particularly dim child. Do I, she asks condescendingly, think I ought to replace certain members of the household staff? Ask, knowing the answer, which members in particular? The Housekeeper, 'not capable of organising a children's tea party' and the entire downstairs staff, 'far too familiar and too much in evidence'. She informs me she is only 'trying to help' and says how Cook, although not of the first order, could with the correct handling be brought up to scratch. She fears my 'soft nature' is being taken advantage of and would I like her to help out? It would be no trouble.

Am given time to think about my reply as HOT coffee and HOT eggs arrive. Agree it would be marvellous if she could help but fear getting replacement staff in the country would prove impossible. Assure her I have tried many times. She taps my hand patronisingly and says 'leave it to me my dear, leave it to me'.

I most certainly will. Finding staff in the provinces is nigh on impossible, I know this for a fact. Even Lady V struggles and she pays her staff. Will await the outcome with bated breath.

When reminded of Strange Odour Housekeeper says she cannot smell anything untoward in the morning room.

August 2nd

Hugo and I ride over to Dear Hattie's where he makes scathing, witty remarks regarding MIL which has us both in fits. He is the master of innuendo and frequently says things in such a way that even if MIL were present she could not possibly take offence at anything he says. I like him more and more each time we meet.

August 3rd

When walking in the summer garden feel confident I know Hugo well enough to ask him about more personal subject. Hitherto we have not ventured beyond casual 'drawing room' conversation and witty banter but feel I want to ask him more direct, intimate question. To this end ask why an erudite, interesting man such as himself has never ventured into matrimony. At first he makes an offhand flippant comment; says that is why he is cultured and appealing because he does not have a wife who would try to change him. When I press further he has a rare moment of seriousness and tells me he has simply never met the right lady. He quickly reverts to type and says if only *I* was available he would not hesitate to ask for my hand. He adds if only I had an unmarried sister. Point out I do, but when Hugo recalls Georgie he raises an eyebrow and declares she is even 'too notorious' for him and that in a year or two she will be 'married to a wastrel spending her dowry as if it is going out of fashion'. See how this is true and that Georgie will be the talk of every drawing room in the country if Mama lets her have her way for much longer.

It is not until later I realise Hugo turned the conversation away from himself by focusing on Georgie in most clever and cunning way ...

August 4th

Housekeeper gives notice.

Ask if she has found source of Strange Odour. She tells me she has not.

August 5th

MIL orders Blake to train the first footman in how to serve at table. The butler seeks an audience with me but in a cowardly act develop a headache and refuse to see him.

Hugo leaves to return to Rudding Park but not before asking Spencer and I to join him for a shooting weekend on the Glorious Twelfth. Am looking forward to it already.

Had quite forgotten Spencer Jnr's new tutor was to take

up his post, so when am told Mr Goode has arrived am quite unprepared. Spencer Jnr makes good first impression by showing new tutor the schoolroom without even being prompted to do so. See how the two of them hit it off straight away which is quite a relief.

August 6th

MIL insists all downstairs maids begin work an hour earlier from now on in order to 'improve and then maintain standards'.

August 7th

Cannot look downstairs maids in the eye but have to admit the rooms are much improved, silver is sparkling and windows and mirrors gleaming.

Note: Strange Odour still in evidence despite new regime.

August 8th

Housekeeper tells me she would prefer not to serve out her notice. She cannot work 'under these conditions'. MIL's new system is 'stringent and unnecessary'. Lower self to plead with her not to go, and offer further financial compensation for her to stay. She reluctantly agrees if I reinstate downstairs maids' original working hours. Am between a rock and a hard place and cannot decide what to do for the best.

Query: Could say old hours will be resumed after MIL departs? Shall try this idea first before submitting to blackmail.

August 9th

Think to escape to Dear Hattie's but on arrival at Highbrow House find she already has a visitor - Colonel Frasier. The colonel, handsome and charming as ever, leaves soon after I arrive but not before he is amusing and extremely flattering to both of us. Military men are always so diverting.

DH and I sit in the garden and drink cordial (laced with spirituous liquor) and eat cake. We discuss Colonel Frasier's merits - devilishly handsome, tall, broad shoulders and sparkling blue eyes. DH says he would be a good match for Georgie if only the girl could be prevailed upon to settle down. Agree wholeheartedly but cannot see how the match is to be brought about unless Georgie pays one or other of us a visit. DH swiftly changes the subject and shows me beautiful diamond and emerald bracelet - a present from The Duke; she has told him her news at last. Feel slight twinge of jealousy, but quickly check the impulse. DH will never have need to sell her love tokens and for this I give thanks.

Tell DH am closer each day to killing MIL. Over the next hour we devise, somewhat childishly, various ways to do this. My particular favourite is poison served in a cream sauce - hot sauce of course. Cannot think how this could be managed without killing everyone else at table. DH stuffs the last of the cake into her mouth (even this action does not render her unattractive) and suggests poison in MIL's breakfast instead. DH points out that as she usually breaks her fast in bed she will die there and so cause less trouble to the servants. How we laugh!

Note: Intend to screw up courage and ask MIL how much longer she intends to stay at Upshot Hall. Need to have hope she will leave before I resort to foul means.

August 10th

Housekeeper still unhappy and so when she offers her resignation (again) in most determined manner am forced to accept it. How vexing this is. I have enough to do without searching for a new housekeeper. Have three months to find competent, hard working woman who is prepared to live in rural location and work for poor wages. Place advertisements but am not at all hopeful of a swift outcome.

Note: MIL no closer to acquiring new servants either which pleases me until see that if she did manage to recruit new staff it would save me the bother.

August 11th

Blake says MIL has ordered him to reduce our monthly wine merchant order by ONE THIRD. This ostensibly because of Spencer's gout. Urgently seek out Beloved Husband and inform him of this outrageous meddling. On occasions have suspected that Spencer has colluded with his mama's intrusive behaviour - anything for a quiet life - but this time see the look of abject horror on his handsome face. He states on no account will he allow this to happen and adds he will speak to his mama without delay.

August 12th

Respite from MIL as we travel to Hugo's country seat, Rudding Park, for the start of the pheasant shooting season. It truly is a glorious weekend (can appreciate not so glorious if one happens to be a pheasant) in which we are treated like royalty, so much so even Spencer who is notoriously hard to please is impressed.

Meet many interesting people and Spencer says the shooting is the best he has ever had. For myself am pleased with all I see. Rudding Park is warm, relaxing and elegant - much like Hugo himself.

August 13th

Splendid day filled with charming acquaintances and superb food. After dinner we retire to Hugo's music room to enjoy musical entertainments - all Hugo's friends are accomplished I notice, including several gentlemen who sing. Am prevailed upon to play the pianoforte and am pleased to say I acquit myself well.

August 14th

Out walking in his verdant park ask Hugo how he comes to have conscientious, hard working staff when the rest of the county struggle to recruit and maintain servants of any calibre. This is a mystery to me as after all he is a bachelor and must rely heavily upon his housekeeper I say.

Depressingly he tells me he pays 'good money'. The solution to our problems at Upshot Hall are, as I suspected, straightforward but unattainable.

Later, mention proposal of raising footmen's wages to Spencer who laughs and asks where do I propose the coin is to come from? Tell him it is false economy not to pay more as I would then spend far less time pacifying the Cook and the Housekeeper. Infuriated when he asks blithely what I would do with the extra time gained.

Husbands can be somewhat exasperating at times.

After this exchange and somewhat alarmingly BH suddenly stares at my wrist. He then lifts my hand so he can see the ruby bracelet more clearly. It is the birthday gift from Fitzroy (who may be dead having fought bravely in some foreign battle or other). Is this new he asks? Am always good at thinking on my feet (another strange saying - thinking on one's feet - why not thinking on one's hands or any other body part?) so quickly persuade him it was a gift from Grandmama left to me when she died. I do not wear it often I explain, as it is quite out-dated. Unfastening the clasp deftly he takes it from my arm and slips it into his pocket as quick as any street slanger. When I ask what he is doing he says if I want to raise the wages of the servants then sacrifices must be made.

Note: Why is it when sacrifices have to be made, invariably it is I who must to make them?

At Rudding Park the time flies by and am able to forget MIL will still be haunting Upshot Hall when we return home.

August 15th

Back at Upshot - Strange Odour still permeating morning room - ask Spencer if he can smell it? He says no then suggests an evening entertainment for his mama - do not suggest knife throwing which is the first thing that comes to mind. Suggest if we make her too welcome it might encourage her to stay even longer. On the contrary, he points out, what he has in mind will be a leaving party. Am instantly cheered until Spencer says the party will not be until two weeks hence. Why wait I ask? He replies that he is hoping to persuade Freddie to invite their mother to stay at Bankwell Hall instead of her spending the entire visit with us. If she does stay on it will not be at our inconvenience (or expense).

Query: Why did she not stay at Bankwell all along? Then we would all have been happy - well not Gwendolyn and Freddie obviously.

Aged Aunt still eating us out of house and home. Had hoped she would have departed by now. The contents of a Welsh mine are used daily to keep her warm only for her to complain of being 'frozen to the bone' at least every hour. In fact have stopped looking at the clock and wait for her to say it is time to bank up the fire. She is like an alarm call and uncommonly precise in her time keeping for one so frail. If one looks closely at Aged Aunt (I try not to look too keenly) one sees there is very little substance to the old dear. She is indeed all bone so concede it may well be her due to complain of the cold. 'Draughts' she says will be the 'death of me'. If only!

Realise it is more expedient to ply Aged Aunt with brandy than keep building up the fires, as brandy sends her into a befuddled torpor thus solving more than one problem. Ask Aged Aunt's companion if she can smell Strange Odour in morning room. She says is it damp?

August 16th

Have decided to 'catch' influenza and have taken to my bed. Or at least that is what I have given out. My nerves cannot stand MIL and her interfering for a second longer; she is too, too provoking. The final straw came when she 'suggested' I ought to have another child 'just in case'. Just in case of what I wanted to ask, we already have a spare, but dared not venture down that route.

Cocooned as I am here in my room, take up Mansfield Park and a large box of chocolates. Am prepared to stay within the confines until the day of the leaving party. Half an hour later Spencer comes and says I must dine with him as he cannot cope alone with the double threat of his mama and the Aged Aunt. Complains that at luncheon Cook served food so hot he burnt his mouth. Explain am far too ill to rise from my bed. He says he is feeling a little under the weather himself now he thinks about it. Ask him to go and be ill somewhere else but instead he takes up Mansfield Park and a handful of chocolates and stretches across the bed and begins to read. After ten minutes he concludes the book is 'unnatural' - (this because it is written by a lady) and asks if I am really ill as to his eye he thinks I look perfectly well. See immediately which way his mind is wandering. Tell him forcibly I am much too poorly to contemplate anything more energetic than reading.

Am relieved when Dear Hattie pays me a visit - on cue as always. Although my Beloved Husband is fond of my sister I feel he finds the two of us undiluted by others hard to handle for some reason. He makes his exit but not before finishing off the chocolates. DH and I spend a happy couple of hours with Bell's Court - *the* most interesting of the magazines to which we subscribe and partake of a fine Madeira.

August 17th

Readdress the fashion section of Bell's and decide Mrs Mary Ann Bell's fashion plates are truly scrumptious. Would Harrogate modiste be able to copy particularly beautiful pelisse? To this end before I break my fast I write to inquire.

Mr Goode, what a pleasant young man, says Spencer Jnr must learn to 'apply himself more strenuously' to his Latin if he is to make further progress. When I tell BH he says learning Latin never did him any favours so I need not worry.

August 18th

Write thank you note to dear Hugo who on hearing I am indisposed has kindly sent over fruit from his hot house.

How thoughtful. Feel somewhat guilty as of course I am not really ailing at all.

August 19th

Spencer bursts into sickroom and drops ruby bracelet on counterpane dismissively. Before I can say how pleased I am to have it back BH glares contemptuously and says he has never been so embarrassed as when pawnbroker told him Grandmama's bracelet was paste. Even goes so far as to almost accuse me of knowing, which of course I did not. Captain Rainer has plummeted in my estimations - silently give thanks did not compromise my honour to the rogue as would feel justified in slapping his face if I had. He is a brigand!

August 20th

The boredom is crippling but refuse to be beaten by MIL - Aged Aunt who Spencer tells me is still in residence has also taken to her bed.

Determine to keep low profile for as long as possible but without visits from Dear Hattie would be driven quite mad.

Of course we discuss the paste bracelet incident at length. DH says she is not at all surprised Captain Rainer has turned out to be a scoundrel. She confides he was definitely encouraging Georgie on her last visit. Indeed she says she caught them, unchaperoned, in the winter parlour and he with his hand on Georgie's waist. When I ask her why on earth she did not think to tell me at the time she gives a plausible excuse; she thought I had enough on my plate so decided to warn our sister off herself. We conclude the man is no gentleman and should he return to these environs - if he has not been killed on some foreign battlefield - then we will not receive him at Upshot Hall or High Brow House.

Spencer, meanwhile, comes to my room most days ostensibly to be ministering to my needs. His mama thinks him over indulgent and begs him to stay away from me in case he catches my complaint. Of course Spencer knows I am malingering but is far too sensible to say so. Not even visit from Treasured Spinster Friend can force me from my room.

After prattling on about nothing of interest she finally gets to the point of her visit; last night's supper party given by Lady V - at least I was spared this. According to her (TSF) Colonel Frasier paid 'wild attentions' to DH all night long. Try to visualise this event but it is beyond my capabilities. She also informs me BH played cards for four straight hours. Clearly she has nothing better to entertain her than to time him. Sadly she was unaware whether or not he was winning or losing. I suspect losing as usual. She also says Mrs Flight (pale blue and cream stripe with long sleeves and lace edged neckline which TSF thought 'too plain') was encouraging Spencer in his endeavours.

Should truthfully feel sorry for TSF - she really must get lonely if all she has to do is watch others and live her life vicariously - but cannot find it in me today. She is a poor sick room visitor; she seldom brings cheer and frequently brings unreliable or tedious gossip.

On reflection feel ashamed of unkind thoughts regarding TSF and vow to make amends - how I am yet to fix upon.

August 21st

After careful consideration think to ask Mama if Treasured Spinster Friend could pay her a visit. It would be a welcome change of scene for TSF. Her uncle must be something of a challenge as he never, to my knowledge, ventures beyond his own fireside. On reflection unsure if Mama would countenance the visit. Last time they met Mama was quite unsympathetic to TSF's plight saying 'she does herself no favours' with her choice of apparel. On that occasion was forced to defend TSF; it is not her fault she has little money with which to dress herself. Even when the uncle departs this world she will be no better off. I believe the house is entailed to a distant male relative. Who knows what will happen to her then?

Will write to Mama nonetheless. Feel keenly I should try to help the less fortunate, especially those with little, or no hope, of marriage.

August 22nd

There is a God. Dear Freddie has persuaded Mother-in-Law to spend the rest of her visit with them. Gwen will be furious - added bonus.

Have miraculous recovery and get up in time to

supervise final preparations for the leaving party. Aged Aunt says thank goodness I am recovered as no one has offered her so much as a morsel to eat or a drink the whole time I have been ill.

August 23rd

Evening entertainment a great success as Mother-in-Law has thoughtfully engineered the whole thing herself so of course it passes without a hitch and with surprisingly little effort on my part.

However, when I see seventy 'friends and family' have been invited, feel a relapse coming on. The spread, the entertainments: theatricals, musicians, ice sculptures, fireworks all put on at MIL's request. Fear the bill will cripple us once and for all. Aged Aunt had to be plied with brandy after fireworks - she was convinced we were being attacked by the French. Aged Aunt vows to go back to Prospect Place first thing. If only.

August 24th

My home is once again my own - except for Aged Aunt who is still sitting on top of the fire like a particularly bony witch. Perhaps she will catch light.

August 25th

Aged Aunt informs me she is to leave after luncheon. She cannot possibly endure another day in this 'ice house'. She is still with us at supper.

August 26th

Pay call on Treasured Spinster Friend and invite her to dinner. She is at once cheered and see how it costs very little to make better other people's lives. Living all alone, except for her ancient uncle, she has very little in life to amuse her. She is to be pitied really.

Note: Must definitely try to include TSF more often in any of our entertainments. Sadly there are no suitors here about who might take her away from all this. At her advanced age (29) I fear that ship has long sailed.

August 27th

At breakfast Aged Aunt's companion thanks me for a pleasant visit but says they are to return home after they have broken their fast. Am cheered to see the coach being loaded with luggage.

Aged Aunt still in residence at luncheon.

Finally Aged Aunt leaves Upshot late in the afternoon. Instruct servants to open every downstairs window in celebration. If I had a flag I would wave it.

Note: Strange Odour in morning room has DISAPPEARED.

August 28th

Float around my home as if on air now it is once again my very own domain. Gather servants together and offer reward for their perseverance of extra sixpence in their wage and a half day holiday when the local fair comes in a week's time. Remember then the Housekeeper problem. Cannot understand why I have not had one single application for the post.

Hugo's words spring to mind but refuse to acknowledge them.

As Spencer is dining out invite Treasured Spinster Friend to Upshot to dine and we have jolly time gossiping about the residents of Killinghall, especially those we do not like (Lady V first and foremost). She is invariably condescending to TSF solely on the grounds of her unmarried state, a fact that is mortifying to TSF and to me too when I come to think of it. What, I say indignantly, would the world be like if we all looked down our noses at *widows* (this just before I slide off the sofa, which granted does not add gravitas to my point).

After dinner we drink a fine tawny port then TSF tells me confidentially how she has met someone whom she 'admires greatly' but knows the gentleman to be 'beyond her reach' despite him showing her his attentions.

Am all amazement at this disclosure and agog ask her what the gentleman has said to make her think he is an Admirer. Am dying to ask her who this gentleman is but try to bide my time - I know from experience she is wont to clam up when pressed too hard.

When TSF is somewhat vague (as is often the case) try to coax her to recall what was said *exactly*. Blushing, she says she cannot recall any *precise* examples but knows he is fond of her. Frustrated, say being 'fond' of someone is not to be confused with other more serious emotions. Dying to know who the gentleman can be as am being driven out of my mind with curiosity, yet at the same time try to assume complete indifference. Ask does she presume he has serious intentions but to this she is silent for some time. She then whispers, 'Sadly not'. Feel like throwing arms in the air dramatically but manage to restrain self.

After this announcement TSF is infuriatingly silent on the matter even after I attempt to bribe the information from her. Conclude it must be Harris Waverly, but how could it possibly be? He is handsome Artistic Type and far too sophisticated for TSF. In addition he cannot be more than two and twenty.

Cannot recall going to bed.

August 29th

Wake with a slight headache and recall conversation about TSF having found an admirer. It is a strange and wondrous concept to think of her in this new light. Never have I known her to voice her admiration for any man (except for Spencer of course but he does not count). Also remember (and feel ashamed) trying to bully her into telling me the name of the gentleman.

Spend rest of morning and much of the afternoon racking brain to think who Unknown Admirer can be. Only wish Spencer was here to ask his opinion. Occasionally, oddly enough, BH is surprisingly perceptive in such matters

- was it not he who first saw the red headed offspring of two black haired friends was a cuckoo in the nest?

Later all thoughts of TSF's Unknown Admirer firmly expelled from head as that evening almost find *myself* mired in controversy.

As Spencer was away overnight on 'important estate business' the opportunity to catch up with Gerald materialised which almost led to a mortifying catastrophe. During my recent incapacitation our local MP was thoughtful enough to send (via Agnes) some especially fond words and so I was more than happy to receive him again.

Wore the paste sapphires he 'gave' me and was relieved to see he was none the wiser the sparklers were not the originals - had thought to wear a particularly revealing gown so as to distract his eye elsewhere. Absence had indeed made Gerald's heart grow fonder. I was presented with a little something to cheer me up - opals. Am touched by his generosity and think to reward him enthusiastically, when out of the blue and inconveniently Spencer returns - this at a *most* inappropriate juncture. Quick thinking required but thankfully BH expertly dealt with by Gerald.

For an awful moment feared a duel would be fought for my honour, but being a member of Parliament Gerald is a consummate liar and soon has Spencer eating out of his hand. He explains all, by saying so convincingly I almost believe him myself, that I am in a state of *dishevelment* because I have suffered a relapse and we were afraid the fever had returned. He explains how he was about to send for my maid to assist him. Spencer, thankfully, is at once pacified and insists on sending for my doctor.

Note: Was in truth thrilled to think a duel might have been fought over me. Does this show me up to be somewhat vain?

August 30th

Over breakfast (where I reassure Beloved Husband I am fully recovered thanks to the doctor's ministrations) ask Spencer why he returned home unexpectedly the previous night. At first he tells me it was on account of him missing me - this I dismiss as nonsense. When I tell him so he is forced to admit this to be an untruth, then says the reason for his return was because he harboured suspicions, 'you were up to no good'.

When I am at first astonished then tearful and then pretend almost to swoon, he is at pains to reassure me he now sees his error. At once he becomes contrite and apologetic. Goes on to say thank goodness our local MP was with me when I suffered my relapse ...

Mem: Write to Georgiana and tell her she will not be received at Upshot Hall again until she writes to Spencer telling him her comment about my questionable reputation was blatant lie. Fear her misguided remark has awakened suspicions in BH.

Spencer, I strongly suspect, is playing some sort of double game. He will need to be far cleverer than he is to fool me. Who exactly has given him his marching orders making him return home with his tail between his legs? Rest assured I shall find out. How dare she? Spencer may be many things but he is *my* husband and I resent any lady who has spurned him. Besides I need him occupied, for without his little adventures Spencer would notice far too much of what happens on his own doorstep. BH needs his diversions to keep him interesting, without them he would drink and gamble his entire life away and then where would we be?

Bankrupt.

August 31st

Spencer sulking about the house in most inappropriate and trying manner.

September

September 1st

Dear Hattie asks me to accompany her to Harrogate. With the atmosphere here somewhat strained am only too pleased to accept her offer. Tell her of recent troubles regarding Spencer and Gerald. She agrees BH is up to something because he knew my illness was feigned. She also agrees it would have been absolutely thrilling if a duel had been fought over me. After some thought she then adds that the outcome of the contest might not have been so exciting if one of them had been terribly wounded or even killed. Concede she has a point. We are however, of the same opinion that had swords been chosen then Spencer would definitely have been the victor as he was school fencing champion at school. Alas we will never know.

Discussed Treasured Spinster Friend's plight with DH and she says why not invite TSF to join us? DH knows she does not get to Harrogate often and thinks it will be a treat for her to mix in wider circle. My sister is uncommonly generous and thoughtful. She will make an excellent mother.

September 2nd

Theatre in Harrogate with Dear Hattie, William and TSF.

Spy Duchess of Lancaster in the box across from us with Hugo in attendance. At the interval he pops in and suggests we meet for a ride in the morning. As always am happy to oblige.

September 3rd

Lovely early autumn day. Dear Hattie, William, TSF, Hugo and I take constitutional ride on the Stray. As always Hugo on excellent form. Notice how he tries hard to draw TSF into conversation but to my surprise she is polite but somewhat cool and dismissive towards him. Why I cannot begin to imagine. TSF is unfathomable.

The thought occurs to me that DH will soon not be able to ride out; her condition is beginning to show. I shall miss our rides but suppose we shall walk instead which to my mind will not be as agreeable, especially as the days turn cooler.

Return to Upshot Hall by late afternoon to find Miss Fairly complaining that Darling Daughter Clemmie will not practise her scales without complaint. Have words with the child regarding her attitude to her studies. 'Can I have a kitten?' is her response.

Words fail me.

Decide against asking Spencer as fear he will say no - again.

September 4th

Dear Hattie is once again suffering sickness in the mornings and cannot keep food down before three in the afternoon. Without her morning calls am forced to make more myself.

Visit Treasured Spinster Friend with intention of resuming our recent discussion regarding her Unknown Admirer - am beyond desperate to know who he can be - she gave absolutely nothing away at Moorlands. On arrival at Spruisty Manor am told TSF is out. When interrogated further the servant becomes flustered and says his mistress is away from home until tomorrow which is even more curious in light of our recent conversation. She had not mentioned an engagement and she *always* tells me when she has received an invitation as it happens hardly ever. Walk back home musing on this mystery.

September 5th

Am even forced to venture to call upon Lady V twice in the same week when all other acquaintances have been exhausted - most are out of town I note. The lady has had a letter from my mother-in-law thanking her for her 'enduring friendship' and saying how 'marvellous' it was to see her when she was in Yorkshire last month. Cannot think of suitable reply so say nothing.

Do I know, Lady V says, (over excellent almond cake) that Mother-in-Law is the most wonderful of women? She goes on to give various examples of MIL's wondrous nature all of which I cannot believe but nod in agreement nonetheless.

We discuss the latest craze for the colour chartreuse, exchange local news (the vicar's wife is expecting her eighth) and the outrageous idea that I should consider sending Darling Daughter Clemmie away to school. Lady V then says in her opinion Dear Hattie is looking 'most unwell'. The state of impending motherhood does not suit every lady she adds knowingly. Had she ever had a child then she knows she would have positively bloomed. Say my sister and I are alike as I too suffered the same fate (sickness morning, noon and night) when in her condition. Lady V says she recollects I was 'quite pasty' each time I was with child. Just how sharp are the knives at Upshot Hall one wonders?

September 6th

Call on Dear Hattie who is decidedly washed-out and wearisome. Sympathise and suggest dry biscuits but feel helpless to do more. Say, uselessly, that the feeling will pass after the third or fourth month. DH is not cheered by this last remark and so to distract her tell her all I know about Unknown Admirer of Treasured Spinster Friend - which is nothing of import really and so takes no time at all.

Spencer and I are to stay at Moorlands tomorrow night as he has a meeting with his broker. Says I need not come (quite irritably in my opinion) but always grasp any opportunity to be in town. Spencer says he will not be able to spare the time to entertain me. Tell him if I relied upon *him* for entertainment then my life would be dull indeed. I ignore the withering look which is hurled in my direction.

Mem: Send note to Hugo to let him know I will be in town tomorrow - now he *is* an entertaining gentleman.

September 7th

Moorlands. Could hardly believe my own eyes this afternoon! Spencer caught with (of all people) Mrs Flight (burgundy stripe with short puff sleeves). The Lucky Widow is indeed lucky to solicit the attentions of my husband. Manage dignified exit to our rooms where I awaited some sort of explanation.

Beloved Husband does not appear until almost suppertime and then is not a jot remorseful. By way of justification says it is not as if I am innocent - what about Captain Rainer? I reply with a well aimed crystal perfume bottle and its contents. Much to my amazement (and distress) it catches Spencer hard on the left cheek. Who would have imagined I was so good a shot? Consider whether I too should take up archery - truth be told was aiming for his shoulder - he should not have ducked.

Blazing row ensues. I point out if he is going to carry on with a lady then choose one who is at least pretty. Heated insults are further exchanged until footman says guest (Hugo) has arrived and is waiting in the drawing room. Spencer shoots me a telling look but say (provocatively) he is being ridiculous - Hugo is an acquaintance *not* a lover.

Cut to Spencer's cheek explained away by saying a tree branch caught him when out hunting. Look on Hugo's face tells me he does not believe it for a second. Spencer looking daggers at Hugo all evening; what our other guests thought one can only imagine.

September 8th

Upshot Hall. Beloved Husband and I are cordial with each other in company and not on speaking terms when alone. Cannot explain why BH is so moody as this is not the first time we have had a problem - just the first time I have caught him in compromising position. He is usually much more careful than that.

Mr Goode begs interview regarding Son and Heir's general lack of progress. Says this is not because the boy does not possess a brain but because he does not 'take readily to his studies'. Goes so far as to suggest Spencer Jnr's father should be consulted. Fear this will only make matters worse. Once again feel hectored into making decisions others are paid handsomely to undertake. Must I do everything?

Later, ride to Dear Hattie's. We discuss the state of my marriage. We agree Spencer is devoid of taste to be carrying on with *that* woman. Also agree it is a reflection on one's spouse who one chooses to fraternise with. In Gerald I at least picked the most handsome, influential man in the county, (after Spencer, William and Freddie). Not that BH thinks Gerald is any way in the picture of course.

DH and I are of the same mind; we deduce Spencer is sulking not because he was rumbled but because of with *whom* he was caught. Of all the ladies in the environs why choose *her* we chorus? DH assures me 'she is not a patch on you'. I, quite cross now, propose that his eyesight is defective.

How we laugh.

DH (still somewhat queasy which means I eat all the biscuits) says ridiculous Spencer suspects entanglement with Captain Rainer. Does he not know he left the district with his regiment weeks ago? Why he cannot see what is in front of him she adds is most odd. Say firmly it is because Gerald and I are far more discreet than BH at hiding trysts.

We eventually come to the conclusion men are indeed strange creatures and go back to trying to think of the name of the gentlemen with whom Treasured Spinster Friend may be embroiled. Yet again this takes no time at all as we are unable to supply ONE SINGLE NAME. DH goes so far as to suggest she is 'making it up' to get attention. See on reflection this is unkind thought but put it down to DH's condition. Know all too well how being with child can be more than trying on one's nerves.

The latest fashion paper arrives from London as we chat so the rest of visit spent appreciating new, low cut necklines. DH declares one of us should be the first to wear it as we both possess the figures to carry it off. I expect it will be her unless some miracle happens regarding my own finances.

September 9th

Spencer still behaving badly and in decidedly odd humour.

Blake tells me the New Housekeeper will arrive tomorrow. Also says departing Housekeeper is awaiting a reference and asks will I furnish her with one? He says this as if nothing could interest him less. There is no love lost between the pair I suspect. Tell him am only too happy to do so now she will be soon someone else's responsibility. Write glowing report to give to her tomorrow.

September 10th

Housekeeper's parting shot as I present her with reference is that I should 'keep an eye on Blake'. In her opinion he is 'shifty' and a 'drinker'.

September 11th

Spencer comes to me and says he has 'given up' Mrs Flight, not that anything inappropriate was going on in the first place he hastens to add; it was a mere diversion, a little flirtation. Was it his fault Mrs Flight misread his intentions? Did I not know after all these years he was faithful to me?

Query: Did he call her by this title during the throes of passion? One would hope not?

Take this to be an apology for his unusual lack of taste. I do believe Spencer was only having a small dalliance with the woman - this sort of thing has happened many times before of course. He has always been a most determined flirt but is far too lazy to take matters further. BH is a handsome man but an idle one. I am well aware ladies have a tendency to throw themselves at him, but also know he lacks the staying power needed to conduct an affair. He has always lacked the wherewithal to cover his tracks; he cannot sustain interest in the pursuance - he is of a similar mind when hunting foxes. Any lady imagining Spencer would make her even a small commitment would be sadly disappointed - he simply does not have the imagination to be properly unfaithful, which to my mind is a blessing.

And besides, he loves me to distraction.

September 12th

By way of further apology Spencer presents me with an adorable white fox cape. Decide to forgive him.

Reconciliation cut short when Gerald calls unannounced.

September 13th

Blake tells me the New Housekeeper has arrived and that he doubts she will be up to the job as she has 'airs'. Decide to withhold judgement until I have at least met the woman.

Hear from Lady V that Duchess of Lancaster is to pay a visit to Knox Park for a week. This is not news as Gerald informed us yesterday when he called to invite Spencer and I to dine when she is in residence. Do not tell Lady V this information and feel justifiably smug.

September 14th

Meet with New Housekeeper who says she will soon have Upshot Hall 'running like a well oiled machine'. Inform her

I was unaware Upshot was going to rust. She has given notice to two footmen and 'has an eye' on Blake. Fear we will soon be fending for ourselves at this rate.

Blake has been the butler here at Upshot Hall since long before my marriage to Spencer, so what he can possibly have done to upset the new broom I can only speculate. Need not have speculated for long; she was quick to tell me her view. 'Drink' she announced ominously and 'back pocket business'. Would not be surprised if Departing Housekeeper and New Housekeeper's paths have crossed. When pushed further New Housekeeper tells me she suspects he is 'under the influence' by midday and is given to taking 'backhanders' to supplement his income. When asked from whom he would receive monies, New Housekeeper is less certain. 'Merchants' she says broadly. Have urge to warn Blake she has him in her sights.

Pay call on Treasured Spinster Friend who again is from home. Her footman says I have just missed her and she has gone to visit the vicar's wife not ten minutes ago. Cannot cross-examine her in front of the vicar's wife so decide will leave note asking her to call on me at her earliest convenience.

September 15th

TSF calls looking decidedly shifty and says she spoke out of turn; she does not have an admirer of any sort. Exasperated at time have wasted thus far so let the subject drop. Should have known there was no truth in the matter. Conclude Dear

Hattie was correct when she said TSF was 'making it up' to get attention.

September 16th

Receive news Aged Aunt has taken to her bed. Doctor says she has suffered a heart stroke and is not long for this world. Spencer pays her a call and solicits information from the doctor. BH is advised she certainly will not linger for long.

September 17th

Aged Aunt remains at death's door.

September 18th

Aged Aunt rallies.

September 19th

Aged Aunt receives another visit from Spencer.

September 20th

Aged Aunt suffers relapse.

September 21st

Make visit to Aged Aunt (deep navy blue with long sleeves, high neckline and suitable sombre expression) and am amazed to see her sitting up in bed eating peaches. The doctor says it is a miracle. Return home and tell BH of state of affairs. He says nothing then leaves the room slamming the door behind him.

September 22nd

Aged Aunt sends for Spencer but he cannot be found ANYWHERE. In his stead go to Prospect Place and sit by bed and keep vigil. Fear I will become a puddle on the floor as the heat is stultifying. The fire is constantly banked up, the windows kept tight closed and her bed heaped in blankets. She must think she has already died and gone to Hell.

The doctor says it cannot be long. Pray her suffering ends before I perspire to death.

September 23rd

Hear from Aged Aunt's companion that Gwendolyn made long visit last night. Freddie is away on business but has been informed of his aunt's condition. Sister-in-Law NEVER visits Aged Aunt.

September 24th

Aged Aunt sends for her man of law. Why? Cannot help but worry she will change her will at the last possible moment. To do so would jeopardise our entire future. Strongly suspect Gwendolyn to be behind this, if it turns out to be the case will never forgive her.

September 25th

Aged Aunt receives visit from Spencer who is at last found. Cannot bring myself to tell BH that her lawyer was with her for TWO hours yesterday (this according to companion).

September 26th

Aged Aunt lapses into state of unconsciousness. Freddie and Spencer keep watch by her bedside. Cannot help but think this is too little too late - where was Spencer when she was conscious? Had Spencer been by her side when she was compos mentis outcome of her will would not now be hanging in the balance.

September 27th

Aged Aunt opens her eyes, tells Freddie he has always been her favourite nephew, and then breathes her last.

September 28th

Spencer inconsolable - and not entirely with grief. We both see how our futures could have been snatched away before our very eyes. Spencer and I discuss state of affairs after he goes to see Freddie. BIL is sanguine and says he knows Aged Aunt will not have changed her will in his favour. Adds she always said Spencer would be sole beneficiary because he was impoverished second son of her darling brother. Only wish I shared Freddie's optimism. In light of this Spencer urges we stay positive but I can see he is much concerned, as well he might be. It is not only our future but that of Spencer Jnr and not to mention Darling Daughter Clemmie - where will monies for her dowry come from if not from Aged Aunt's coffers?

Worry drives us both to drink far too much wine at suppertime.

Mr Goode comes to see me (as if I do not have enough to be concerned about) and says Spencer Jnr refuses to study; Son and Heir says he should not be expected to be at his lessons during period of mourning. Tell tutor to disregard son and carry on as usual.

September 29th

Spencer tells me mourning black suits me. Tell him I think it washes me out but am grateful for the compliment nonetheless. Little embellishments such as jet beads help to draw attention from severity of black Agnes says. I agree wholeheartedly.

Spend morning happily making lists of ways to splurge the money Deceased Aunt will have left us. Spencer warns not to count our chickens but argue surely she will stay true to her word ... cannot put thoughts of deathbed change of heart from my mind. Still dare not mention a word of lawyer visit to Spencer whom I fear is already spending on account.

September 30th

Can hardly sleep for worrying in case Deceased Aunt has indeed changed her will. Could cheerfully murder Gwendolyn - thought of being disinherited at the last hurdle is all too real and too cruel to contemplate.

Worry is driving me to drink.

October

October 1st

Deceased Aunt's funeral. Interment takes an age then half the county gather, including Hugo Bright, at Prospect Place; twenty bedrooms, Palladian style filled with ugly, dark furniture and ancestral paintings by the yard. Deceased Aunt had the most unprepossessing relatives which I suppose are Spencer's kith and kin too now I come to think of it. Thank God he did not inherit the family chin. If we do indeed come into this pile it will take some restoration to make it comfortable. Still at least it is not damp - the interminable fires have seen to that.

Internment followed by reading of the will. Give huge sigh of relief when man of law declares, as promised, all Deceased Aunt's worldly goods are to go to Spencer. This includes Prospect Place and all its acres, farms and pastureland, a townhouse in Richmond, another in Whitby and more stocks and shares than one can shake a stick at - What does that mean exactly? Why would one want to shake a stick at anything?

I neither know nor care. My joy is boundless.

Beloved Husband composes face into suitably dour,

dignified expression.

Later Hugo says saucily how he sees I will never leave Spencer for him now. Say au contraire I will cause scandal and leave with all the money. We both laugh raucously then realise we are at Deceased Aunt's funeral wake. Duchess of Lancaster frowns in our direction.

Just as am about to corner Treasured Spinster Friend am waylaid by Gwendolyn who says, quite spitefully in my opinion, she hopes we will be happy now. What an extremely rude and hurtful thing to say! Cannot think what I have ever done to deserve Sister-in-Law's disapprobation. It is true I made no secret of the fact before she married Freddie that I thought he could have done better. Without her substantial dowry I doubt he would have even given her a second glance. Notice even in mourning garb the woman is dressed inappropriately. How Freddie puts up with her is beyond me. He is always so well turned out and she is always dressed in frills and flounces like a young girl at her first ball.

Query: Did Freddie ever tell Gwen how we were once quite fond of each other in the past? As this was before his marriage I would think it unlikely, but men are odd creatures and Freddie is like a loyal spaniel where his wife is concerned. Could this be the source of her disapproval?

See TSF leave with Lady V, the vicar and Hugo. The hangers on are hard to dislodge even when all the food has gone.

Back at Upshot Hall Spencer and I crack open the

champagne and give thanks for the Deceased Aunt's frugal lifestyle. Begin planning three month sojourn abroad for the winter which will thankfully, necessitate a whole new wardrobe.

Also plan redecoration of Upshot Hall to take place whilst we are abroad. Yellow paint ordered for the withdrawing room along with yards of peacock blue silk to re-upholster the chairs and sofas. At last feel light of heart and free of financial load. What a relief it is to know all our futures are now safe and secure.

October 2nd

Spencer insists we undertake a period of three months mourning out of respect for Deceased Aunt. Three months! Agree to compromise on two months after I point out Christmas in a state of mourning would be completely unbearable.

Note: Beloved Husband looks handsome in black. The thought of dour looking apparel for the next two months will be trying for me but as Agnes points out it will not be forever. She urges me to order new outfits as way of compensation.

October 3rd

After further deliberation about length period of mourning should take, Spencer announces one month will be sufficient. This after he realises there is a race meeting at York he would miss if two months is adhered to.

October 4th

Summon Cook and with the greatest of pleasure serve notice on her. Celebrate with a small sherry.

October 5th

Lady V drops in and tells me about rumours regarding Mrs Flight which she cannot even begin to countenance. This begs the question of why she is repeating the rumours in a house in mourning does it not? Consider this in very bad taste but it is only what I have come to expect from her. She has it on good authority, whose she cannot divulge, that Mrs Flight is carrying on with ... Spencer arrives at just this very moment bows low over her fat fingers and then continues to play up to Lady V rendering her insensible. She tells him he is a 'naughty boy' (!) to say she looks so young and adorable. Cannot meet his eye; his behaviour is ridiculous in the extreme and demeaning to all present. Spencer, unusually when Lady V calls, stays to tea and flatters her so much she is quite as pink as a blancmange by the time she leaves.

Query: Why, ask self, when ordinarily Spencer cannot stand to be in the same room as Lady V does he loiter like a bad smell?

October 6th

Beloved Husband failed to return home last night (will remind him if he ever returns he is supposed to be in mourning). This after we have blazing row over his outrageous behaviour with Lady V. The argument starts when I tell him it is mortifying to both myself and him that he suddenly and incomprehensively flatters Lady V so shockingly. Ask what can he be thinking? Of course Spencer cannot supply reasonable grounds for his extraordinary attentions. When he tells me he does not have to explain himself to *me* I become exasperated and turn on my heel and make a dignified exit before I say more than I should.

Later Dear Hattie calls and tells me he was playing cards with William until the early hours. William says Spencer was losing heavily at whist and faro when last seen. No surprise to me at all. A fool and his money are soon parted. Fear inheritance has gone to his head.

October 7th

Decide mourning attire adds at least a decade to my age. Black does not suit me in the least, despite what Spencer says. Urge Agnes to embellish clothes somehow but know that strictly speaking jewels must be kept to a bare minimum; only being able to wear jet is becoming tiresome and it is hardly becoming to any young lady of fashion.

Spencer still not surfaced. Last seen at his brother's house where according to the oracle (Gwendolyn) he was 'the worse for wear in drink and sleeping it off after another night at the gaming tables. Notice how Gwendolyn came to call solely to tell me this news.

No doubt BH is running up debts on the strength of Deceased Aunt's legacy as probate still pending.

When Gerald called to see me last night was reduced to telling him about BH's behaviour. Gerald and I are in agreement Spencer really is inconsiderate to say the least. Know it to be the height of bad manners to discuss a spouse's faults with an *amour* but this is the depths to which BH has brought me.

October 8th

Spencer returns looking as if he has not seen a bed in a week. Takes to his rooms and is not seen until suppertime when half a dozen of his least respectable cronies arrive to sup. They then retire to the library and play cards until Lord knows when.

Seldom have I been so disenchanted with Spencer. I at least, am following the convention of mourning and Deceased Aunt is not even a blood relative of mine. Even a fine sherry cannot lift my spirits. Fear for our future if this is how Spencer is to behave. We will be ruined before we know it and not just financially.

October 9th

Decide after careful consideration to confront Spencer in his rooms. This state of affairs cannot continue. Ask if he is intent on steadily working his way through Deceased Aunt's legacy by recklessly gambling it all away? Say had hoped newly acquired fortune would be put to better use than gambling. Try, and am pleased to say I succeed, in making BH see that the welfare of his family, especially Son and

Heir, should be paramount. After much blustering he admits he has been rather free with his coin but says he intends to mend his ways from now on. Agrees it is true he has been a little carried away since financial burden has been lifted. He immediately begs my forgiveness which is most unlike him. Only time will tell if he stays true to his word. Feel somewhat anxious we will never achieve solvency as Spencer has little business sense and only a thin grasp of self control where gambling is concerned.

October 10th

Order two new gowns, three pairs of slippers and a mink muff while I still can.

When Dear Children are brought down in the evening Darling Daughter Clemmie says how she misses Deceased Aunt dreadfully. Spencer Jnr then adds he misses her too. Am astounded as did not know Dear Children had contact of any note with her. On the contrary says Miss Grimes, Aged Aunt was in the habit of spending at least an hour with the children in the nursery every day when she was staying at Upshot Hall. Miss Grimes then astonishes Spencer and I by saying she and the Dear Children called at Prospect Place every week at Aged Aunt's request. Later, Spencer and I conclude we did not know Deceased Aunt at all. BH says he is touched and vows to adhere to protocol of mourning period more strictly from now on.

October 11th

Spencer says he has 'urgent business' in Harrogate and is not seen for the rest of the day.

October 12th

Beloved Husband presents me with diamond pendant and matching earrings, brooch, ring, and bracelet! Am stunned both by the extravagance of the gift and the brilliance of the stones. Suspect these to be peace offering but as yet am unaware of what he has done to need to require forgiveness, besides gambling excessively of course. Surely he cannot have worked his way through Deceased Aunt's legacy before it has even been banked?

Panic begins to set in.

At wit's end so decide to ride over to Bankwell Hall and speak to Freddie. Tell Brother-in-Law of financial fears. Freddie, as usual, is ready to reassure and says he has advised Spencer on a number of issues regarding his inheritance. Am relieved beyond measure to hear it. Says he has directed BH to put monies in trust for Spencer Jnr until he reaches his majority. Plans have already been set in motion to this end he adds reassuringly. A substantial amount has also been set aside for Darling Daughter Clemmie's dowry, a fact which pleases me beyond measure. Freddie tells me he has also suggested to Spencer that Prospect Place be let on a long lease to provide a steady income. The land is already let to tenant farmers and will also furnish us with revenue. Who would have thought BH would turn out to possess the sense to listen to his brother?

Am much relieved and on my return feel it only right and proper to forgive Spencer (some of) his misdemeanours. We make up and together continue to plan the itinerary for our winter trip abroad. Italy will be a firm destination needless to say. My only regret, and it is a large one, is that Dear Hattie and William will not be able to join us because of her condition. Nevertheless am sure it will be the trip of a lifetime.

Query: Still unsure why Spencer was so keen to play up to Lady V. Fear it is one of life's little mysteries I must learn to live with.

October 13th

Marital harmony once again re-established. Am still finding black very trying but now Spencer is conforming to rules of mourning feel it is a burden shared. Mourning is a tedious time and without Dear Hattie for company would be driven insensible.

October 14th

Dine with Freddie (and Gwen) - mourning black but still she is resplendent with lace cascading like waterfalls from her neck and wrists; she puts me in mind of a particularly bad tempered crow. Freddie, so handsome and urbane, is such a good husband yet Gwen appears hardly to notice him at all. How does she manage to hold onto him? Later when I mention thoughts to Spencer, he astounds me by saying to his knowledge Freddie has never strayed. Not once. This I find truly astonishing. The man is a saint.

October 15th

Am intercepted by New Housekeeper on way to break my fast. She feels she has to tell me Blake needs to be dismissed. She cannot of course serve notice on the butler herself, so asks if I will do the necessary deed. Remain firm and say I will not as he has been loyal and faithful servant for over twenty five years. New Housekeeper then threatens to give notice but see immediately how this is idle threat.

Tell Spencer about how New Housekeeper feels regarding Blake remaining in post. He says on no account can we part with 'trusty old servant' and that he would rather be rid of New Housekeeper. Wholeheartedly agree on both counts. Besides, much like Agnes, Blake knows too many of our secrets.

Note: The Cook's offerings since she is working her notice have, strangely, been of a higher standard than at any time over the last eight years. Servants, much like men, are hard to fathom. Just when you expect them to behave in a certain way they do the exact opposite.

October 16th

Spencer and I dine alone and actually enjoy a quiet evening at home.

October 17th

Walk around the garden nearest the house and together Spencer and I plan improvements to include the widening of the turning circle, a large impressive fountain, and new wrought iron gates to be fixed into new tall perimeter wall. The latter will afford us much needed privacy. We agree it is entertaining to spend time together deciding upon enhancements to Upshot Hall. After a splendid supper we have an early night - the second this week.

October 18th

Have finally, after much soul searching, divined reading is not a pastime that comes easily to me and have vowed to give it up completely (all except for fashion magazines of course). The 'Literary Lioness', Walter Scott, et al are not my cup of tea. And as for poetry, hell will freeze over before I read another stanza.

When footman brings the latest edition of The Lady magazine (this periodical indeed lives up to its name - Entertaining Companion for the Fair Sex), along with a warming drink, I notice something familiar about the man. I look again and am convinced - if I am not much mistaken the new footman is the old footman, Frost/Forrest. Summon New Housekeeper who says she has indeed hired two new 'experienced' footmen to replace the two she dismissed. Frost/Forrest it appears is one of them. Am reminded of a weather clock I once saw where on the hour a figure of a man comes out of one door and returns via another. New

Housekeeper says the New Cook has arrived. Would not be at all surprised to see it is the old Cook just wearing different garb.

October 19th

With little to occupy me and mourning still dragging on, begin to plan house party for the beginning of November to signal the end of our period of respect. Forty guests, twenty of whom will be staying at Upshot Hall, are sent invitations. Have avoided hosting too many house parties in the past mainly because of the burden of expense such entertainments incur, but admit am enjoying the idea of having friends to stay. Now Upshot is resplendent and The New Cook at least appears capable, feel confident it will all go off swimmingly.

October 20th

The house party will be New Cook's first challenge - hope it will not turn out to be a disaster and she lives up to my expectations. Ask to see New Cook ostensibly to welcome her to Upshot Hall but also to set boundaries. See now how I allowed Old Cook far too much leeway which led her to believe she could hold me over a barrel all too frequently.

Query: Is New Cook far too young to be in charge of a large and busy kitchen? Pray fervently she is up to the task ahead.

October 21ˢᵗ

House in uproar as rooms are readied and servants are sent forth with more purpose than have ever witnessed before. New Housekeeper knows how to crack the whip and entire house is as clean as a new pin. Never seen the chandeliers, mirrors and silver sparkle so brightly.

New Cook says sample menus are well within her capabilities - trust she is right.

October 22ⁿᵈ

Luncheon late being served as Blake says New Cook struggling with ovens which refuse to get hot enough. When food finally arrives it is at least edible. In fact Spencer goes on to say it was delicious. Will not give up praying that house party runs smoothly just yet as there is still the matter of the ovens to take into account.

Spend anxious afternoon convinced tonight's dinner will be served at midnight? Tell New Housekeeper to press New Cook to consider next few days a test of her competency.

October 23ʳᵈ

Am touched when Spencer presents a large box which clearly contains a new gown. He says, smiling boyishly, that it is an end of mourning offering. How thoughtful. He knows how much I have detested wearing black. The gown - rose pink figured silk - is exquisite and he tells me he has had it sent from London. It must have cost a small fortune, but agree when he says I deserve nothing less.

October 24th

New Cook serves dinner two hours later than planned as ovens still proving a trial. Forty guests will be arriving tomorrow and am now in state of panic in case she is not up to the job. For once Spencer sees the urgency of the problem and despatches handyman to kitchen to 'sort the stoves and ovens out once and for all'. Throw myself into his arms and kiss him (Spencer's arms, not the handyman's).

Spencer declares Upshot Hall has never been so well run and declares he is proud of me. Says he is looking forward to the house party enormously.

October 25th

Guests, including the Duchess of Lancaster, begin to arrive for house party. After our guests take luncheon (food arrives hot and on time) the gentlemen leave to go fishing. After bracing walk in the grounds we ladies join them at our fishing lodge. All in good spirits as the River Nidd, which passes through our park, is teeming with trout; this means the men have had a profitable afternoon which makes them all the more amiable.

Over delectable (intentional) cold collation sent to lodge by New Cook we discuss the King's latest problem and the state of the highways. Splendid time had by all.

Treasured Spinster Friend is tight lipped when I eventually corner her and beg she share with me the name of her Unknown Admirer - am convinced she has one even though she now denies existence of such a gentleman. Short of pummelling the information from her am uncertain what else to do.

First night dinner a triumph. Not only was it served on time, each course was more mouth watering than the last. Generous compliments from all guests - regular visitors most effusive of all in their praise. Even Lady V can find nothing of which to complain. Great relief all round.

Had thought to invite Hugo of course and as always find him to be charming and amusing dinner guest. Am a reliable judge of character by and large but tend to see only the good in people which may be a fault as from time to time one is let down. Not so with Hugo Bright. After supper he tells me he is something of a gourmet and what a relief it is now I have a decent cook. He says he has never before tasted syllabubs quite like mine. Tell him I am most gratified to hear it and we both laugh like little children until the Duchess of Lancaster casts a stern glance in our direction.

Had placed Hugo by Treasured Spinster Friend at dinner; they have met before of course but hoped she would find Hugo more entertaining than the last time they met. He reminds me of a benevolent uncle and had hoped he would prove to be an amusing companion for her. TSF, inexplicably mute as far as I could tell throughout twelve courses. The woman is beyond understanding.

Later, introduce topic of TSF's Unknown Admirer with Hugo - restrain self from apologising for saddling him with her at dinner - vow not to foist her upon him at any future gatherings. He foolishly suggests I pin her to the floor and tickle her. He says if I did that to him he would tell me anything I wanted to know. He is so droll.

Conversation turns to travel and Hugo tells me he is to return to Italy soon. When he did his grand tour he enjoyed the country very much he confides. Tell him how I long to learn the Italian language so that I may converse with the locals on our visit next spring. 'Adorerai le persone' he says expertly, which he says means I will love the people. Might have known if any of our circle could speak the language it would be Hugo! Why had not thought of him I cannot speculate. Beg him to teach me a phrase or two of *Italiano*. Concentrate hard and finally grasp two short speeches but fear using them in company. Feel sure they are not as innocent as he says; suspect they may well be quite rude.

For the rest of the evening watch TSF like a hawk - what I expect to uncover have no idea - none of the guests would be remotely suitable for her - too rich, too handsome or too urbane. Conclude Unknown Admirer must be someone from out of town if indeed he exists at all

October 26th

Whilst perusing the shops in Killinghall all thoughts of Unknown Admirer put from head when I bump into Captain Rainer (had not even known he was alive let alone back from manoeuvres). With a confident flourish he introduces me to his WIFE. None other than the well dowered Miss Shaw (as was) of Thirsk! Reeling, feel compelled to invite them both to masque ball I had planned later in the week.

Captain Rainer MARRIED to MISS SHAW! Would not be at all surprised now to find TSF is engaged to a groom or a tradesman. The world has indeed turned topsy turvy. Consider whether I am really such a good judge of character after all.

October 27th

Gerald calls and suggests 'we are careful' in light of recent near disastrous episode. Agree completely and go as far as to suggest we might use his return to London to cool things off all together. He says he would regret this but quite sees my reasoning. What a lovely man - enjoy our last leave taking enormously but on reflection have no regrets at the decision.

October 28th

Too many house guests still in evidence. Perhaps open ended invitation may have been unwise. We spend days hunting, shooting, fishing, playing lawn games or shopping depending on our tastes.

Note: New Cook is proving a marvel but see how this is a double edged sword; when Old Cook in residence guests more keen to leave - there is only so long indigestible food can be tolerated.

October 29th

Masque ball to mark end of house party (hopefully lingerers will get the message). New gold taffeta and Chantilly lace looks charming and am not unhappy with general appearance especially when the new diamonds are added to the ensemble. Darling Daughter Clemmie even says I look beautiful.

Masques worn by guests make them appear stylish, sophisticated and just a little intriguing in some cases. Indeed one or two of the gentlemen are positively rakish - have often thought the idea of being held up by a highwayman thrilling. Spencer, in his masque and wearing deep blue is particularly attractive.

Note: Masque worn by Lady V an improvement - should be compulsory at all times. The lady, dripping in sapphires, is all smiles when Beloved Husband kisses her hand. Regret asking the loathsome woman but one can hardly exclude such a near neighbour. Dear Hattie (red watered silk with scoop neckline and puff sleeves) suggests wickedly that Lady V has her eye on Spencer and I should watch out as she has always admired him. Say hell would freeze over before Beloved Husband would ever reciprocate her feelings. We laugh so much it sets Dear Hattie off hiccupping for a good ten minutes.

Notice Statuesque Red Haired Beauty in conversation with Gwendolyn - cannot begin to describe what Sister-in-Law is wearing - a disaster in dark green velvet trimmed with, of all colours, YELLOW. The woman has absolutely no taste whatsoever. Cannot fathom who unknown Statuesque Red Haired Beauty can possibly be. Even when she removes her masque to reveal almond shaped green eyes, I am none the wiser. She is not on the guest list so who invited her to the soiree is a mystery. Spencer, unsurprisingly, is like a moth to a flame. He appears to know and appreciate the lady's charms and is uncommonly eager to dance with her and afterwards show her the conservatory which at this time of year is a dull, cold place. See it must be he who has issued the invitation.

Also notice Dashingly Handsome Soldier wearing uniform of a lieutenant. Am introduced and am told he is the husband of Statuesque Red Haired Beauty newly arrived in the area to take up position at the barracks - the husband not the wife. What an addition to Killinghall he will be. I already have a liking for him especially so when it turns out he is an excellent dancer.

He takes me to one side and boldly asks when Spencer will be from home as he thinks he has to see more of me. Suddenly feel winter will be a warmer affair than had hitherto dared to hope.

Later, back in my boudoir peer at my face in the looking glass with utter horror - am struck how by the end of a party I do not look half as fetching as I did at the start. Wonder if Statuesque Red Haired Beauty has the same misgivings. I fear not.

October 30th

Have spent the afternoon laid down in a darkened room suffering the greatest of shocks. This morning as guests finally packed and readied themselves to leave Upshot I made my way to the hall to bid them *arrivederci*. When passing the morning room I hear voices and thinking I recognise the dulcet tones pop head around the door to see Treasured Spinster Friend in passionate embrace with HUGO BRIGHT! She smiles gaily (not at all the shrinking violet) as Hugo tells me their 'Good News'. They are to be married ... Susan Simmons and Hugo Bright are to be man and wife? *He* is Unknown Admirer!

Words temporarily fail me but then rally and congratulate them with rictus grin pinned to face.

TSF gushes *they* are so pleased I am the first to know as I am so dear to them both. Hugo laughs loudly and says my face is a picture! The Duchess of Lancaster, who was on her way to her carriage, looks in and says 'at last' as if she has known he is Unknown Admirer all along. TSF says I *must* be guest of honour at their wedding. Says how thrilled she is to be able to share her happiness with me now Hugo has done her the honour of asking her to be his WIFE. She adds how they hope to marry as soon as possible and how marvellous it will be to honeymoon in Italy.

See remaining guests off in a haze of confusion.

October 31st

Still reeling from yesterday's revelation. Cannot picture Treasured Spinster Friend as mistress of Rudding Park (and her not being a SPINSTER is even more disarming). Dowdy SUSAN SIMMONS will be mistress of all those acres, not to mention excellently trained servants. And the very thought of her enjoying the sights of Italy before me! Life can often be too, too cruel.

Spencer, who is never here when I have need of him, has once again performed one of his disappearing acts, so invite Dear Hattie to dine. Am keen to discuss the impending marriage of the two people I have long thought of as loyal, close friends.

After I tell Dear Hattie all about it she swears she cannot believe I am telling the truth, then calls TSF 'a dark horse'. Agree completely but say what about Hugo? He is the worst culprit as he never breathed a word even when I told him I was desperate to know who Unknown Admirer could be. Decide he is no longer to be considered a loyal, close friend and that he is old and his eyes are far too close together and this makes him not at all trustworthy in our opinion. Also decide he is marrying Susan Simmons in mistaken belief she will inherit large fortune on her uncle's death. She will not of course and that will serve him right.

Much cake is eaten, not to mention the wine DH and I consume. Eventually begin to feel better about forthcoming nuptials of Miss Simmons.

Note: Must decide upon new monogram for former TSF. Will give this some thought when I have recovered my senses.

Later Dear Hattie says on reflection she is pleased for TSF as state of spinsterhood is mortifying for any woman, and for a plain woman such as her without funds must be doubly so. For myself am still strangely perturbed by the idea of the pair being joined in holy matrimony but expect in time I will come to terms with it. Concede DH's point but say would it have been too much to ask that Miss Simmons trusted me, her oldest friend, with the information? Am I not the soul of discretion? DH thinks for a long moment and then says, 'Not entirely.' At first am affronted at her comment but she goes on to say that had TSF confided in me I would have most certainly told her and also Spencer. Suddenly see the funny side. She is of course quite right but then I add there is one person I would definitely have kept in the dark.

'Lady V' we chorus! Oh, how we laugh.

Dear Hattie, who decides to stay the night, says get into bed for God's sake her feet are freezing. Say gaily I will but am writing my diary. She laughs loudly and in most unladylike manner and says perhaps I should publish it and become famous 'Literary Lioness'.

Climb into bed beside DH with a night cap for the both of us. Tell her I am certainly more of a writer than a reader so who knows what notoriety awaits me.

Dear reader only time will tell.

The End.

www.ingramcontent.com/pod-product-compliance
Lightning Source LLC
Chambersburg PA
CBHW061547210726
48287CB00006B/2105